FLAMES OF FORTUNE

An enthralling novel set amidst the flames of the Great Fire of London

Lucy, the tavern wench born from the flames that destroyed her past, escapes the slums of Restoration London into the household of a merchant and his lovely young wife. Soon she gets caught up in the intrigues of two blades from the dissolute court of Charles II and, amid the crackling inferno of the Great Fire, another child is born.

FLAMES OF FORTUNE

FLAMES OF FORTUNE

Aileen Armitage

Severn House Large Print
London & New York

This first large print edition published in Great Britain 2002 by
SEVERN HOUSE LARGE PRINT BOOKS LTD of
9-15, High Street, Sutton, Surrey, SM1 1DF.
This title first published in Great Britain 2002 by
Severn House Publishers, London and New York.
This first large print edition published in the USA 2003 by
SEVERN HOUSE PUBLISHERS INC., of
595 Madison Avenue, New York, NY 10022

Copyright © 1971, 2002 by Aileen Armitage

All rights reserved.
The moral right of the author has been asserted.

British Library Cataloguing in Publication Data

Armitage, Aileen, 1930-
    Flames of fortune - Large print ed.
    1.   Great Britain - History - Restoration, 1660 - 1688 - Fiction
    2.   Love stories
    3.   Large type books
    I.   Title II. Quigley, Aileen, 1930 -. Child of Fire
    823.9'14 [F]

    ISBN 0-7278-7164-1

Except where actual historical events and characters are being described
the storyline of this novel, all situations in this publication are fictitious a
any resemblance to living persons is purely coincidental.

Printed and bound in Great Britain by
MPG Books Ltd, Bodmin, Cornwall.

X000 000 020 8301

For Peter

CHAPTER 1

"This is the place, I warrant you Roger; Piers said it was hard by London Bridge, did he not?"

The loud imperious voice of the young man who had just entered the inn quelled at once the laughter and talk of the people already sitting, tankards in hand, in the tap-room. Every head turned to survey with interest the handsome young gentleman and his group of friends, pressing and laughing behind him. From the finery of their lace ruffles, it was evident even to Lucy, the kitchen maid, that they were wealthy young men.

"He did, Toby, but I think it was not the Tabard but some other inn that he named," replied one of his companions.

"No matter, we'll just wait here a while, and if he comes not, we'll go seek him elsewhere. Landlord!" The young man and his companions strode to a corner table.

From the kitchen at the back of the inn came a large smiling man, his face ashine with his efforts in the steamy kitchen.

"Good sirs," he said, "I am the landlord, Garth by name. What can I serve you, gentlemen?"

"Bring us a flagon of ale, landlord," said Toby, slapping a gold coin on the table, "and be quick about it." Then he turned and slapped his friend jovially on the shoulder. "Roger, my friend, there is much sport to be found in London tonight. What shall it be first? A wench, eh? Or shall we help the watchman fulfil his duties?"

The group seated around his table roared with laughter at his implications. Lucy, sent by Garth to carry the ale to the gentlemen, could see that this handsome dark youth with his flashing eyes was the centre of the group, the leader of their pranks.

She set the flagon and tankards on the table and straightened up.

"By 'r Lady, what have we here?" said Toby in tones of great surprise. "A lady, a veritable beauty, and in such a place. What say you, Roger? Would not our friend, Piers, be inflamed to paint this creature? She's lovelier by far than some of the wenches whose portraits he's done. Would you like your portrait painted, my lovely?"

He seized Lucy round her slender waist and held her close to his shoulder. Lucy stood still, her face downcast.

"Look on her skin, Roger," Toby went on, "a fine creamy texture, is it not? Not a pock-mark upon it. It goes well with her flaming auburn tresses. What hair! What a strong, silky texture it must have." He reached up to stroke it, but Lucy broke from his grip.

"By your leave, sir," she said in a low, even tone, "can I serve you aught else? Some meat pasty, mayhap?"

Toby looked up at her and answered slyly, "There is much you could serve me, pretty one, but for now more ale will suffice." There was another roar of laughter from his youthful companions, and as she turned to go, he dealt her a resounding slap on her rump.

Lucy, her face flushed with anger, bounced into the kitchen.

"By my troth," she exploded to Garth, "were it not for your kindness to me and the fear of driving your patrons away, I would fain have returned his blow to his saucy face. The others I can handle, but these gentlemen spend well, I know not how to

11

deal with them."

"Gently, Lucy," said Garth in his slow, kindly way. "It's difficult enough for you, I know. Bide you here while I serve them. You can help my wife with the victuals."

By the time Lucy re-entered the taproom some time later, the roysterers were gone. "But the fine young gentleman bid me tell you he would return," Garth murmured. "In the meantime, serve that lone young man who has just come in."

Lucy approached the pale, dark-haired young man who stood just within the door, his eyes scanning the assortment of pedlars, merchants, wherrymen and their women who were now singing and laughing again.

"What is your wish, sir?" she asked him. He looked at her solemnly and said with some asperity, "Has there been a group of young gentlemen here this evening? A gay crowd, probably somewhat heated with wine by now? I was to have met them here-abouts."

"If among your friends there are two named Toby and Roger, they have," replied Lucy, her manner becoming cooler. He did not seem the wanton, reckless kind. His clothes were well cut but more sober, and his manner far more civil than the earlier visitors to the inn.

"Sir Toby, if you please!" His voice was decidedly sharp. Lucy felt stung by this unwarranted reproof.

"I do not know the gentleman, sir. I only heard the names they used to call each other by. Shall I fetch you some ale or a cup of sack, sir?"

"Thank you, no," he said, turning, then paused. "Do you know whither they were bound when they left here?"

"I neither know nor care," replied Lucy, "for I would not wish to pursue any acquaintanceship with Sir Toby."

"Have a care, child, or your manners will undo you," snapped the young man, and he swung rapidly out of the door.

Child, he called her! How dared he! She was sixteen last April, and he was certainly no more than in his mid-twenties himself! She had learnt a great deal in those sixteen years, she reflected. It had not been an easy life, though Molly had done all in her power to bring her up as best she could.

Lucy's face softened as she thought of Molly, the nearest substitute she had ever had to a mother. She could remember nothing of her own mother, only the great, leaping flames remained immovably fixed on her memory; the flames of the fire from which Molly, returning home to Butcher's Row late at night, had snatched the baby Lucy.

"Poor lamb," Molly had often said to her, "robbed of father, mother, brothers and sisters all at one go. They found naught but ashes when the fire died down," and she would tell Lucy how even the neighbours could tell her little about the family who had only just come to live in that little close-packed street, and who had kept very much to themselves.

"It was God's grace, child, that I happened to pass at the right moment, and heard your faint cry. In the smoke I managed to find you, guided by your wail, but the heat was too intense to go in again. By then a crowd had gathered, and they held me back."

This much Lucy knew from Molly. Her own memory, apart from the vision of the flames, extended back only as far as childhood, to playing in the rubbish-strewn Butcher's Row while Molly worked at her washtub, and to eating thin gruel and sometimes vegetables fallen from the farmers' carts, or thrown-out scraps of meat. But behind it all was Molly's warmth and maternal tenderness, her ample bosom always ready to receive and comfort Lucy's childhood woes.

Lucy's reflective train of thought was cut short by Dan, the pedlar, calling for more ale.

"Come on lassie, there's thirsty throats awaiting you," he quipped, and winked broadly at Dr. Augustus, the quack who had been busy all day selling his patent medicines in the little square outside the inn. "Methinks Lucy is in need of one of your nostrums, doctor," he laughed. "Have you a certain cure for love-sickness?"

"Love-sickness? Not I," said Lucy with a laugh. "I'll talk and flirt and be gay with any man, but fall in love, and call him lord and master? Never!"

"You'll change your tune one day," said Dan, nodding his head wisely. "Just mark my words."

Lucy tossed her auburn hair proudly, its glow reflecting the light from the tallow candles. "That will be a wondrous day indeed," she said. "The heavens will rain fire, or the earth open its jaws at the very least, the day I give myself to a man and tell him roundly that I love him," and she bounced back to the kitchen. Garth,

15

standing leaning his heavy girth against the door jamb, his great arms crossed over his chest, smiled as she passed him.

"Nevertheless, little one, the day will come," he said gently.

As the hour grew late and the drinkers, pleasantly sated, made their way home, the taproom grew quiet. Lucy was about to pull her shawl around her and leave, when the door opened again and a plump woman clutching a shabby shawl to her shoulders, hurried in.

"Molly!" cried Lucy. "I was just coming home. Why are you come here?"

"Lucy, my love," said Molly, easing her weight on to a stool for a moment, "I've been all evening with a stranger to the city, a merchant, and he asked me to show him around – to the cockfight, to the pleasure gardens and all, and now he'd fain go home and sup with me. But if you're there, Lucy..." Molly's voice tailed away. Lucy saw her dilemma at once.

"Away with you, Molly," she said lightly. "I'll go sleep on Mercer's stall tonight. He's told me he'll not mind. Go, go home, Molly, before your merchant disappears," she went on as she saw Molly's guilty look. "The night is warm. No harm will come to me."

She smiled as Molly, her lined face softening as the tension eased, hurried out of the inn again, mumbling her gratitude.

Lucy sighed, and after bidding Garth and his wife good even, she too went out into the warm spring night. She walked along the bank of the Thames towards the row where Mercer, the tailor, lived. He had a display stall projecting from the front of his house, and sheltered as it was by the overhanging upper storey of the house, it would afford a comfortable enough place to sleep.

Beggars often slept out at nights on these stalls, and Mercer had offered her the use of his when he found her once sitting outside. By this time Lucy had grown old enough to understand the significance of Molly's nocturnal visitors, and to realise that her absence would be welcome. Odd, she mused as she watched the torchlights gleaming across the river, she had this inborn feeling that she could not willingly give herself to any man, yet she did not love Molly any less because she was a whore.

By the time she was twelve, the Lord Protector's reign had come to a sudden end and Charles was restored to the throne, and with him gaiety and freedom came back to the land. Everywhere she had seen men and women laughing and drinking, and caressing each other since she grew to womanhood. Many men had flirted with her in the tavern, but life had taught her how to deal with importunate customers. A laugh, an impudent quip and a deft manoeuvre out of reach had kept the customers happy and calling for more ale, but she would have to be in sore straits to sell herself for money, she reflected.

This in itself made her feel guilty and unhappy. Only now could she appreciate that the gruel and scraps of meat in her childhood had been bought by Molly's selling herself. It had never occurred to Lucy's child-mind that taking in odd bits of laundry would not be sufficient to feed two hungry mouths, but now she knew and loved Molly the more for her generous love. Molly's admirers may well have been legion a dozen years ago, but now her lined and pockmarked face, laughing and kindly though it was, attracted few customers. Tonight's merchant was the first for many months. Garth had been generous of his kitchen scraps since he'd taken Lucy on, but winter was coming on apace, tavern customers would be fewer, and Garth might well have no further need of her services.

Lucy's reverie was interrupted sharply by the sound of raucous laughter and running feet. Drawing back into the shadow of a house wall, she saw three or four figures running towards the wherry on the river-bank. There they stopped. She could guess by the fine cloaks and air of merriment they were another group of rich young royster-ers, somewhat the worse for heavy drinking.

Another figure ran up and joined the group.

"That will suffice for one evening's sport, Toby," said a voice. Lucy recognised at once the sharp tone of the young man who had come to the Tabard in search of Sir Toby. "Into the wherry. It's time we sought our beds."

"Come now, Piers, you wouldn't have us break up the night's sport when the excite-ment is just beginning," complained the petulant voice Lucy recognised as Sir Toby's. "Did you see that watchman's face?" he continued gleefully. "He couldn't believe his eyes! He agrees to take a cup of wine with us in Blackfriars, not knowing we had administered a little preparation of our own to the cup, and falls soundly asleep in his box. The next thing he knows, he opens his eyes, and heaven be praised! He's in

Southwark! He didn't know he'd slept all the time we trundled him in his box across the bridge!"

Piers and the others roared with laughter at the memory of the watchman's disbelief and horror.

"Perhaps we overdid the jest a little when we overturned him and his box on the ground, and left him struggling helplessly like a turtle on its back. I think it time we went home now, Toby. How say you, Roger?"

"I at least am willing to seek my bed," replied Roger. "Carrying that box so far has quite tired me out." He turned to call the wherryman who was plying along the bank, and in turning, caught sight of Lucy in the shadows.

"Gentlemen," he said. "We have company."

Toby, seeing the girl's figure in the half-light, advanced towards her, lurching as he came.

"Toby," said Piers in a low voice.

"Away," replied Toby. "Here's a maid who needs someone to escort her safely home. You would not have me desert my duty as a gentleman, would you? Come, my lady, you'll be safe with us," he urged her, drawing Lucy out of the shadow.

The moonlight fell full on her upturned face and her large, expressive eyes.

"By Jupiter! It's the maid from the inn!" exclaimed Toby. "Piers, it's the pretty wench I told you you ought to paint! Do you not see – no, the light is not enough to do justice to her skin, her hair. Such fine features – I'd swear she is no gutter wench! We must take her to where there is light to see."

"I have seen her," replied Piers. "Let us go."

"We must take her with us, then," argued Toby. "You'd like that, wouldn't you? How are you called, little one?"

"My name is Lucy. If you please, sir, let me go," said Lucy, trying to disentangle her arm from Toby's grip.

"No, hang it. I'm sure you'd prefer my house to your own," said Toby in a petulant tone again. "Come with me, Lucy, I'll look after you. You shall have a pretty new gown and venison for dinner. Wouldn't you like that?"

"In return for what payment?" demanded Lucy, "for I am certain that you will demand recompense."

"She's a sharp one, is she not for one so young?" inquired Toby of Roger with an admiring smile. "How old are you, Lucy?"

"Sixteen, sir."

Piers, who had been pacing impatiently between the group and the wherry, stopped suddenly.

"Enough. Away home, Lucy. Goodnight," he said quietly. "Come Toby, the wherry-man waits."

"Let him wait," roared Toby and clutched at Lucy's shoulder for support as he swayed drunkenly again. His eyes glistened as he felt the firm young flesh under the thread-bare woollen cloth of her shawl, and he kept his arms about her. "She shall come, will you not, Lucy?" he said softly, urgently.

"For a meal and a warm bed I will come," she answered levelly, "for bed I have none tonight. I shall repay you with whatever work you may find to give me, but I will share my bed with no-one."

"You're wasting time, Toby. Let her go," said Piers again.

"I'll take her – on her terms too," laughed Toby. "Mayhap she will change her mind when she finds she has a liking for venison, a soft bed and a linen gown."

Laughing softly, he helped Lucy into the wherry, and Roger and Charles followed. He did not see the determined set of her

small, defiant chin, but Piers, sitting opposite her, was watching her closely and
scowling.

CHAPTER 2

On the further bank of the Thames the group were unable to find a hackney carriage, one of the innovations in London life since Charles had ascended the throne. Toby claimed he had a filthy headache and felt sick, anyway, and the thought of riding in a bumpy carriage over uneven, rutted roads made him groan, so he suggested that they should walk. Lucy was sorry she could not experience the thrill of a coach ride at least out of her impulsive decision to go with Toby, and was beginning to regret having made the decision at all. Piers walked, his head averted, deep in his own thoughts, and it was left to Roger and Charles to talk to Lucy as Toby's groans grew louder with every step. Finally Roger and Charles parted company from them, and Piers was obliged to support a tottering, moaning Toby along the road.

Outside the gate of a large house, standing

back in its own ornate garden, Piers stopped and propped Toby against the gate pillar.

"Where are we?" moaned Toby, blinking blearily round him. Lucy stood back, forgotten for the moment.

"Kempston House," replied Piers. "I'm home. How do you feel, Toby?"

"The fires of hell are burning my brain and my stomach," said Toby feebly. "For pity's sake Piers, let me stay with you the night."

"Indeed," agreed Piers. "My brother would gladly give you bed and board, but what of your doxy?"

Toby's eyes tried to focus as he made an effort to understand what Piers was saying, then without a sound he suddenly crumpled into a heap on the ground, completely unconscious.

Piers sighed. "Give me a hand, child," he said. Lucy hurried forward and struggled to help him raise the inert Toby from the ground. "Now ring the bell," he ordered.

She did so. "I shall go now," she said, and turned to go.

"Come here. You came hither on the promise of a bed and a meal, and those you shall have," Piers said curtly. She followed him in as the porter opened the door.

"But it is not..." she began.

"Be silent. I am too tired to argue with you. The housekeeper will see to your wants." His voice was abrupt, sharp and would brook no denial. Lucy felt angry. He was not offering her a bed out of kindness to her, but only to discharge a debt of honour on his friend's behalf. She could acknowledge his loyalty to Toby, but could he not be more gracious in his manner?

He disappeared upstairs, bearing Toby's now snoring figure with the porter's help, and left her standing in the vestibule. Lucy gazed in awe at the marble figures in the niches of the wall, and after some minutes, feeling she had been forgotten, she turned to slip quietly out of the door again. A woman's footsteps clattered on the floor behind her, and she turned.

"Come this way," said a birdlike little woman, and before Lucy knew it, she was downstairs in the kitchen, being ordered to peel off all her clothes and take a bath. "Can't have you soiling our fine linen," said the brisk little creature.

For the first time in her life, Lucy bathed. After the initial shock of total immersion, she began to revel in the luxury of the feeling, then of being towelled vigorously.

By the time she was led to a cot in the maid's room, in the attic, she was feeling quite sleepy. Heaven, she breathed as she lay in a cotton shift between cool sheets, heaven could be no more blissful than this. And I share my bed with no-one!

She woke early to find the little woman standing over her.

"Come now, dress quickly, the master is waiting to see you," she said briskly, and held out a woollen kirtle to Lucy.

"Mr. Piers?" asked Lucy.

"No, Mr. Thomas, his brother," replied the woman.

"That's not my gown," said Lucy sleepily as she rose.

"I know. We were obliged to push yours on the fire – torn, it was, too far gone to repair. Be grateful, child. Put it on, hurry now."

Mrs. Platt, as she told Lucy she was named, led her downstairs and announced her. "The young maid Master Piers brought home sir, Lucy," she said, and pushing Lucy into the room, closed the doors behind her.

Lucy was aware of a vast oak-panelled room with heavy furniture, gleaming brass and marble statuary. But the focal point of the room was the vast desk, behind which sat a middle-aged man with thinning hair and spectacles, peering closely at some papers in his hand. Beside him stood a pale, slender girl of about her own age, a girl of delicate peachlike beauty, cradling a white kitten in her arms. She smiled gently at Lucy, then lowered her gaze, and Lucy was fascinated by the childlike face, the soft, rounded cheeks suffused by a gentle blush. How clean, how shy and graceful she looked, in contrast to the girls Lucy had known all her life.

The man at the desk looked up and smiled at the girl beside him.

"Forgive me, Elizabeth, I was totalling these costs. What was it that we were to discuss?"

The girl put down the kitten and nodded shyly towards Lucy. "There is a maid who waits to speak with you, Thomas. Our business can wait a little longer."

"I had forgot. Well now, what is your name, child?"

"Lucy, sir." She curtseyed.

"What is it you wish, Lucy?"

"Nothing sir, I was bidden to come to you. Your brother was kind enough to give me a night's lodging."

"Piers did?" said Thomas, his eyebrows arching in surprise.

"Do not misunderstand, sir," continued Lucy, "he did it only to oblige his friend, Sir Toby."

"I see," murmured Thomas, but he sounded puzzled still.

At that moment the doors opened and Piers entered, heavy-eyed and vexed, and behind him came a huge bull mastiff. Piers flung himself into a chair, neither looking at Lucy nor speaking to her. The dog crouched obediently at his feet a moment, then suddenly stiffened and growled.

"Quiet Prince!" Piers said sharply, but the dog continued to growl. The kitten, coming out from under Thomas's desk, arched its back and hissed, and the dog started menacingly towards it.

"Oh, Snowball!" Elizabeth cried in alarm. The tiny creature spat defiantly at the dog, then turned tail and ran for the velvet drapes covering the window, its feet slithering on the highly polished floor. The dog snapped at its hindquarters and the kitten squealed in terror as it clawed in vain at the drapes, unable to get hold and climb out of danger. Elizabeth stood white and motionless, her hands to her face.

Quickly Lucy cut between the dog and the kitten and snatched the little thing up in her arms. She felt its claws sink into her forearm as she held the stiff little body close to her.

"How dare you sir!" Piers snapped to the dog. "Outside!" He held the door open and the dog, reluctant to end the sport, hesitated before he slunk out.

"Oh thank you!" Elizabeth cried as she took the kitten from Lucy. "Thank you so much." Piers turned to Thomas.

"I must explain about the maid, Thomas, lest you misunderstand," he said curtly.

"There is no need, Piers, the child has told me you acted on Toby's behalf," Thomas interrupted. "Where is he now?"

"He is ill in bed," Piers answered. "He can remember nothing of last night. I shall send him home in the coach later in the day."

"It's about time that young man learnt to stand on his own feet," Thomas commented drily.

"Then I'll get rid of the girl," said Piers, rising from his seat.

"Do not trouble yourself," said Lucy, feeling that they were speaking of her as if she were not there, as of a disobedient child. "I can betake myself to where I came from. Thank you for the bed and gown, and if I am under no obligation to you, I will go."

"Hold hard!" said Thomas. "No need to

be offended, young woman. If you have been led hither under a misapprehension, the least we can do is to make some amends to you. Mrs. Platt will give you a good breakfast, and money and victuals to take with you."

"Let her go," said Piers. "She's benefitted already from her trip even if she did not get her whore's fee from Toby. She's cleaner and better dressed than when she came."

"Whore indeed!" Lucy snapped, her green eyes flashing with fury. "You do me wrong, Master Piers! I have starved and frozen many a time, but traded my virtue for food or clothing, never! Do you know what hunger and cold signify? I'll warrant your belly has never ached for whole days together, nor have you slept out at nights under a blanket of frost. If you had, you'd think kindlier of those who are forced to give their all, in order just to stay alive. But thanks be to God, I have not yet been obliged to go a-whoring for money."

She glared at them all defiantly, her head held high. In silence Piers regarded the floor.

"Bravo, my child," said Thomas. "But do not think unkindly of us. I'm sure Piers did not mean to be so unfair. If he does not choose to do so, I apologise for my brother's behaviour."

"Thomas, may I speak with you?" Elizabeth's gentle voice cut in meekly.

"Surely, my love," Thomas answered, and led her to a window seat in the corner. Again Lucy felt unsure what to do. She had not finally been dismissed, but she felt it would be uncouth simply to turn and go. Piers looked up.

"Have you eaten yet, Lucy?"

She shook her head. He opened the door and held out his hand. "Come."

Very stiff and erect, she passed him and he followed her out.

"I'm sorry," he said abruptly as they walked along the corridor. "I misjudged you. Take this." He held out a gold coin.

Lucy looked down at his outstretched palm, then slowly up at his face, a clear head above her own.

"I accept your apology, sir, but not your money," she said with dignity, and walked on. He hurried after her.

"Please, I must do something to atone," he said, "if not money, then what? Have you no hungry brothers or sisters it may help to feed?"

"None, sir," she replied, then a vision of

Molly's lined face came up before her. "Yet ... yet I could make use of it well."

"Then take it," he said pressing it into her hand. "And is there aught else I can do?"

"Thank you, no," she smiled. "This will take care of the next few weeks, and by then mayhap I shall have found fresh work to do."

Lucy's natural high spirits began to return. "In our way of life," she went on, "we can only look to the present, something will always turn up for the future."

Piers left her with Mrs. Platt and after Lucy had eaten a meal of bread, meat pasty, ham and a tankard of ale, he re-appeared.

"Come," he said simply.

Back in the study, he bade her be seated on a leather chair, then left. Elizabeth was seated on a joint stool near Thomas, who was again busy at his desk.

"Lucy, my dear," he said, "are you employed to work at this Tabard?"

"Yes, sir, at the present I am a serving maid there."

"I see." Thomas rubbed his chin thoughtfully. "Would you consider taking employment here as a maid?"

Lucy looked at him, then at Elizabeth, who smiled shyly.

"You see, Lucy," she said. "I am in need of

a maid, and I fancy perhaps you and I could suit each other admirably."

"My wife has taken a fancy to you, Lucy, and that's the truth of it!" said Thomas fondly. "And I am loathe to deny my pretty little wife anything her heart desires."

His wife! Lucy was stunned. She had taken Elizabeth for his sister, possibly even his daughter, but that she should be his wife had never crossed her mind for a moment. She looked such a child, younger by far in worldly wisdom than Lucy herself. The world was full of wonders.

"You hesitate – does the idea not appeal to you?" asked Elizabeth, a disappointed look on her face.

"I'm sorry, I was thinking," replied Lucy. "Indeed the idea appeals to me greatly, madam." Elizabeth's look changed to a smile of pleasure. "In truth, I think my work at the Tabard cannot last much longer, and I should be glad to work for you."

It was true. There was something so innocent, and appealing about Elizabeth that Lucy felt she would be glad to serve her and protect her. Strange, she thought, that they had both felt a simultaneous attraction to each other, when their lives, their upbringing and their natures were evidently so different.

"Good, that's settled then," said Thomas with a businesslike air. "Now you two can get along and discuss the details between you while I return to my accounts."

As Elizabeth took Lucy by the arm and led her towards the door, it suddenly opened and a lovely dark-haired girl somewhat older than themselves burst in.

"That stupid Platt!" she exclaimed, giving Lucy a cursory glance, then addressing herself to Thomas. "She knew I was going riding this morning, but she let me sleep till now before waking me with my breakfast. Do you think I could have the carriage, Thomas, to get me to the riding academy? Monsieur Foubert will be so cross if I am late again."

Elizabeth drew Lucy out and closed the door softly.

"My husband's cousin, Rebecca," she answered Lucy's unspoken question when they were alone in Elizabeth's room. "She has been brought up with Thomas and Piers since childhood. I rather think she resents my intrusion since I came her a few weeks ago. I must explain," she went on shyly. "You must deem it odd of me, but I am a stranger in London, I've never been far away from my home in Northumberland until now, and there was something in your manner that made me believe we could be friends, you and I."

"But madam, I am only a serving maid," replied Lucy in surprise. "We have so little in common, you who are so gently nurtured and I."

"Please, not madam. I beg you may call me Elizabeth, and count me your friend. I am in sore need of friendship, Lucy." Her eloquent eyes were large with pleading.

"But your husband – Mr. Thomas – he is very concerned for your wants and your welfare," said Lucy, puzzled. It had been obvious from Thomas's gentle, considerate manner towards Elizabeth that he cared deeply. What need had Elizabeth of a girl like herself as a friend, when it would seem she had everything?

"Thomas – yes, he is very kind. But I do not know him yet, Lucy." Elizabeth turned and gazed out of the latticed window as she spoke. "He has only been my husband for the past two months. Before that, I lived very quietly with my mother in the north. My father died six months ago. You may have heard of him, Lord Sherdley. My name is Lady Elizabeth Sherdley, or rather, it was.

Now I am wife to Thomas Armytage, merchant of London."

She turned and sat by Lucy on the window seat. With downcast eyes she went on. "It is not easy for me to talk of my inmost secrets, but I do not feel you are a stranger, Lucy. Times were hard for my mother after my father died, and she determined to provide for me, her only child, as best she could. So when Thomas sued for my hand, she was happy for me, for now I should want for nothing. To Thomas, I am an ornament, a prized possession, someone he can introduce with pride to his friends as, 'My wife, the Lady Elizabeth'. It is good for business, but I am sure he will treat me with kindness. My mother made one stipulation out of concern for my youth – that after our wedding, Thomas should allow me to travel for six months before making me truly his wife, and he agreed. Now preparations are being made for my departure – and yours too, Lucy, if you will come. You will, won't you, Lucy?"

She gathered Lucy's hand into her own. "I need you, Lucy. I'm sure you can appreciate my position. I need your strength to bolster my own weakness."

Lucy smiled. "You do yourself wrong,

mistress. You are no weakling, of that I am sure. But I should be proud to be of help to you. If you would permit me first to return to Southwark and tell my friends, Garth and Molly, of what I am doing, then I shall be free and willing to come."

Elizabeth's eyes shone. "Dear Lucy. I sensed it from the moment I saw you that you had compassion for others – and then you saved my kitten. I shall order the carriage to take you to Southwark – then hurry back. Oh!" Her eyes clouded. "I'm sorry – Rebecca is using the carriage..."

"No matter," replied Lucy. "I prefer to walk as I am accustomed."

As Elizabeth accompanied her to the door she added with a smile. "You see, Lucy, we had more in common than you thought; we were both virtually friendless."

"And as you are still a virgin wife, we have that too in common," Lucy laughed. Elizabeth held out her hand shyly, and Lucy clasped it heartily. "I shall return soon," she promised.

CHAPTER 3

There had been a heavy rainfall during the night. Lucy picked her way carefully along the muddy street, not wishing to soil the hem of her new gown, or the shoes Mrs. Platt had given her. It was rather uncomfortable to wear shoes for the first time in her life, but it was one of the arts she would undoubtedly have to learn for her new way of life.

Southwark looked incredibly dirtier than it had ever appeared to her before. It was the contrast between it and the beautifully clean and well-appointed Kempston House that showed it up so abysmally. As she neared Butcher's Row, threading her way between the rotting piles of refuse and evil-smelling dungheaps, she wondered how Elizabeth or Rebecca would regard this place, with its squalid, close-packed wooden houses whose upper storeys almost met across the street. Little air or light penetrated this place.

Rebecca, she felt instinctively, would curl a contemptuous lip and make some sneering comment. Elizabeth had implied, discreetly, that she and Rebecca were not close friends, otherwise Elizabeth would have no need of a pauper serving maid like herself to befriend her.

A sudden cry of "Mind yer 'ead!" made Lucy start. A cascade of water crashed to the ground before her, missing her by inches. She looked up to see the gnarled face of an old woman at an upper window grinning mischievously.

"Fine lady like you shouldn't be walking hereabouts," she cackled and withdrew. Lucy laughed inwardly. Even old Mother Paxton could not recognise her with months of grime washed away and a fine new gown. The appearance of a well-dressed woman had brought out her resentment; Lucy hoped her new-found luck would not alienate the affections of the rest of her kind, the people amongst whom she was born and bred. Her sudden rise to fortune, going to work amongst the rich, might anger and estrange them, but not Molly or Garth, surely. Suddenly she felt uneasy. It was hardly kind to tell Molly, living in all her wretchedness, of her own luck. Garth would be happy for her, but he was comfortably enough placed, with the inn making his life secure. But Molly ... that was a different matter.

Lucy loitered at the end of Butcher's Row. It was no use, she could not set off on her travels with Elizabeth without seeing Molly again and telling her what had befallen. Molly was her mother in all but the physical fact of not having given birth to her. Had she not told Lucy that she had even suckled her, having lost a babe of her own only days before? He had been one of the many babes Molly had borne or miscarried in the course of her work, and not one of them had survived the first year of life.

"A groat, my lady, a groat will provide an old soldier and his family with a fine meal, the first for weeks," she heard a gruff voice at her elbow. She turned and smiled mischievously at the man in tattered uniform, leaning heavily on a crutch.

"Go on with you, Edgar, you have no family but your doxy in Cades Place. And I saw you only last night eating a hearty meal of pasty in the Tabard."

The soldier looked at her quizzically, then his eyes widened. "By 'r lady, it's Lucy, is it not! I scarce could recognise you in your finery." He smiled.

"You sly old dog, Edgar. You know you earn far more as a ruffler than ever I did at the Tabard! Put your good leg to the ground, or you'll be getting cramped!" She chuckled as he did so. "I must admit, you're very convincing, but I know from your own lips you never saw service on any battlefield. Tell me, have you seen Molly today?"

"She was at the Tabard this morning, fetching food and ale for her gentleman friend. For aught I know, she's at home still," Edgar replied, and strode away.

At the door Lucy hesitated, then knocked. There was a scuffle and a sound of murmuring voices, then Molly's head peered round the edge of the door.

"Yes? – oh, Lucy – a moment, love." She disappeared and a minute later she emerged, red-eyed and blinking in the broad daylight, and closed the door quickly behind her.

"Sorry love, I couldn't let you in. 'E's there yet, and likely to remain some time. A day or two, with any luck. That's if you can..." Her voice tailed away as her bleary eyes accustomed themselves to the light and she caught sight of Lucy's appearance.

"My, ain't you fine?" she murmured in

admiration. She pulled a slipping shawl back up over her flabby shoulders, the white scars left by the pox gleaming against the surrounding grey skin. " 'Ad a bit of luck, 'ave you? You look fair pretty, Lucy. Doesn't seem five minutes since you was a baby, and look at you now, as pretty a maid as ever I did see. I shall be losing you one o' these days when some young gent takes a fancy to you."

Lucy threw back her head and laughed. "He'll have to be a very special man ere I take a fancy to him," she chuckled. Then she grew more serious. "Molly, I may be going sooner than you expected." She walked along the Row, her hand cupped under Molly's elbow, and told her of the events of the previous night.

"I like this maid Elizabeth immensely, and I feel I could be of help to her, but I hate to leave you so."

Molly's eyes narrowed. She shook off Lucy's hand from her arm and turned to face her.

"What do you mean? You're not doing me any favours by staying, my girl. On the contrary, the sooner you go, the sooner I'll be free to be my own mistress again."

Lucy looked at her in shocked surprise.

"Molly, you aren't telling me to go, are you? That you don't want me here any more?"

"Don't take a hint easy, do you? I've looked after you long enough Lucy, it's time you went out into the world and took care of yourself," Molly said emphatically, crossing her arms and pursing her lips.

Lucy's lips trembled. "I'm sorry, Molly, I had no idea. Forgive me for burdening you so."

She turned away, ashamed of the tears trembling on her lashes. Many had scorned and reviled her in the past, but no-one had ever pierced her armour as Molly did now. She remembered the gold piece in her pocket – Molly should have that at least.

She pressed it into Molly's resisting hand. "I cannot find the words to tell you how I feel, but thank you for everything. I shall try to send you more money from my wages."

"Don't trouble," Molly said abruptly. "I shall manage better alone."

"I hope we shall meet again," Lucy muttered hoarsely. Tears were blinding her eyes now as she turned and ran along the street, no longer avoiding the puddles.

Lucy sat for a long time on the river bank watching the wherries and the barges passing by, and trying to fix the point on the skyline where Kempston House lay. The air above the city, however, was one long pall of smoke, caused, so she had been told, by the sea-coal the rich folk burnt on their fires.

Finally she made her way to the Tabard Inn. Garth was glad to see her, and bid her go through to his wife in the kitchen, who would see she had a meal of the leftovers from the roast beef they had been serving.

"Thank you, but I have eaten well today, Garth," Lucy said, and went on to tell him of the offer Thomas had made her. "So if you would be pleased to get me to go, I shall be well provided for," she finished.

"Well, I am pleased, and that's the truth," said Garth with a broad smile, "for you know I could not employ you for much longer. Go to your new position, Lucy, and good luck go with you."

Relieved that she was free to go, Lucy sped back across London Bridge, trying to put out of her mind Molly's sharp dismissal. Molly, the only person who had ever truly loved her and sacrificed all for her, nearly her life even, had told her she was unwanted and sent her away. That hurt her deeply. Then suddenly, she realised – Molly had made one more sacrifice. Lucy's tears flowed freely until she reached Kempston House.

She found Elizabeth in the kitchen with Mrs. Platt, supervising the unloading of a number of hampers.

"Just look, Lucy!" she cried in delight, "fresh fruit, vegetables, peaches, quinces, asparagus, and a turkey – and here's eggs! Oh, this does remind me of home!"

"From the market?" asked Lucy; the odour of fresh fruit was mouth-watering.

"No, from Longacre, Thomas's country house near Gloucester. Mrs. Platt has vegetables sent from Covent Garden and poultry from Leadenhall, but Thomas prefers his own country-grown produce, and he's had his servants send these up to us."

They left Mrs. Platt to continue unpacking. Satisfied that Lucy was not hungry, Elizabeth took her to her room. "Now, we have much to discuss," she said, as they sat in the window. "First, Thomas tells me the arrangements have been made for us to leave for France in six weeks' time with Mother Benson, his old nurse. We shall travel to Dover by coach, and there take sail for Calais. Then we shall travel by coach again to Paris. How do you feel about going abroad, Lucy? Are you excited?"

Lucy smiled. "Indeed I am. But coming to live with you in your way of life is a whole new world to me in itself. But what of you? Having just left your mother to face life in London, does the prospect of going to France not frighten you, Elizabeth?"

"Travelling there does not affright me, not with Thomas to guard us as far as Dover. Of course, he may have to go to York on business soon, but if he is away, then Piers will escort us."

"But will not this journey interfere with Piers' work?" Lucy asked Elizabeth. "I imagine he does work?"

"No," answered Elizabeth soberly. "He was at one time employed in the business with Thomas but found commerce not at all to his liking. Buying and selling wool meant little to him. He is far happier with his oils and canvas, so in time Thomas decided Piers was better employed painting than in the office. And really, Thomas is so rich there is no need for either to work. Thomas goes on negotiating his business in this country himself because it is a game of wits to him, a challenge that he enjoys for its own sake. But he does not care for foreign food and the poor man gets terribly seasick, so occasionally Piers goes abroad on his behalf."

Elizabeth jumped up and took Lucy's arm. "Come, I'll show you some of Piers' paintings."

Lucy followed her to the gallery running along the head of the main staircase. "There," breathed Elizabeth softly.

Lucy saw a row of portraits, one of which she recognised as a profile of Thomas, in which Piers had accurately captured the far-away look of pre-occupation in the gentle grey eyes, and one of Rebecca, striking and dramatic with her jet-black hair and flashing brown eyes. There was a self-satisfied curl at the corners of her lips, and a proud, con-temptuous look in her haughty eyes.

"They're very good – life-like," com-mented Lucy. "I wonder he has not done one of you."

"He has not known me very long," said Elizabeth, blushing, "but he has begun a series of sketches in order to do my portrait one day. Come, we must go through my wardrobe. Thomas says I must have new clothes for the journey." She cast a glance over Lucy. "I think you and I are of a size, Lucy. Mayhap you would like to have a few of those gowns I no longer need. Then I shall order a cloak for you too when we visit the dressmaker tomorrow."

She was like a child in her enjoyment of life, Lucy reflected as she followed Elizabeth back to her room. No-one could help liking her. Elizabeth was already at the press, pulling out gowns. She held one of green satin up against Lucy.

"Oh Elizabeth! That's far too fine for me," said Lucy, laying it on the huge, canopied bed. "What need would a chambermaid have of such a gown?"

Elizabeth's eyes were wide with dismay. "Oh Lucy, I haven't offended you, have I? I would not for the world hurt your feelings. That plain dark worsted you are wearing now suits you admirably; it sets off the glorious colour of your hair to perfection. But if you are to be my friend as well as my maid, Lucy, there will be occasions when you will have to accompany me to where a finer dress than a maid's gown will be essential."

"What kind of occasion?" asked Lucy, mystified.

"Well, walking in the Park, shopping, riding – oh, a dozen things. And Thomas says I'm to be presented at Court before I leave England. I shall need to have my maid with me at Court, to arrange my dress and my hair for me. So you see, you must accept."

Elizabeth had a way of making it sound as if Lucy were doing her a favour, and Lucy was grateful to her. In Lucy's life up to now, people were not given to being so tactful.

"Thank you," she said simply.

"It is almost time for dinner," Elizabeth went on. "You will eat with Mrs. Platt and the others, and I shall look forward to seeing you again after dinner. Go to your room now and prepare." She pressed the gown into Lucy's hand as she spoke, and opened the door.

Lucy slipped out and began to hurry along the corridor to go down to the servants' quarters. As she passed an arched doorway near the head of the staircase, she was startled out of her wits when a strong hand suddenly shot out and gripped her by the wrist.

"What's this? Thieving – and in broad daylight? And from your benefactors too? How dare you!"

Lucy looked up at the face of a very angry and indignant Piers.

CHAPTER 4

"What are you doing here still?" he demanded, keeping his grip firm on Lucy's arm. "I thought you had returned to Southwark this morning. And why are you creeping away from Lady Elizabeth's room, her gown in your hand?"

"By your leave, sir," fumed Lucy, wrestling her arm free. "I am Lady Elizabeth's maid, as of this morning, and I have this gown with her consent. Ask her if you will!" She glared at him defiantly. Yet again he had presumed to attack her honour, and once again without reason. Creeping indeed! What kind of a sly, cunning creature did he take her for?

"Is this true? Is that why my brother sent for you to his study this morning?" Lucy nodded, tears of anger making it difficult for her to speak.

Piers hesitated for a moment. "I'm sorry, Lucy," he murmured. "I seem to be making a habit of misjudging you. If you are to live here, I hope we shall not continue to misunderstand each other. Please forgive me for jumping to a not altogether unwarrantable conclusion. I should like us to be on good terms."

Lucy bit back her tears and looked at him solemnly. He was smiling at her gently. He really could be most charming when he shook off his abrupt, stern manner, she decided.

"You are to be Lady Elizabeth's maid, you say?" he continued when she did not answer him. "Did my brother say whether you are to accompany her abroad shortly?"

Again Lucy nodded.

"I see. Well, I daresay Rebecca will be pleased about that, as she will now probably be absolved from accompanying Elizabeth and Mother Benson. She made it quite plain that this was a task not to her liking at all."

He smiled and made to go.

"A moment, sir," said Lucy quickly. "You are right, Master Piers, it would be best if we understood one another. We both have something in common – our concern for Lady Elizabeth. Thank you. I should be glad if we were friends."

"Then there's my hand on it!" laughed Piers, holding out his hand, like one man to another. Lucy put her small hand in his firm grip, and he shook it, the smile still playing round his mouth. "And now, to your work, my girl," he said, and went back into his room.

Lucy's hand still tingled from his grip. She felt embarrassed at the handshake; he had been teasing her, playing with her as with a child, she felt sure. He was determined not to take her seriously, it seemed, except at the moments he had believed her to be dishonest. Each time she met him, the interview left her uncomfortable afterwards. Why should it matter so much to her that Piers should think well of her, she wondered.

She reached the servants' hall to find the staff scurrying to serve up the family's dinner. "Make haste," Mrs. Platt was saying to the little serving girl, Jennet, "or Miss Rebecca will make your ears ring if you're late with the soup."

When the family's meal was over, the kitchen staff gathered at the deal trestle table in the middle of the vast kitchen to eat. Gradually, as they devoured the pigeon, beef, cabbage and the pudding left over from the family's dinner, Lucy learnt that apart from Mrs. Platt and Jennet, the other staff were the woman cleaner, the laundress, the gardener, and the coachman cum porter who had helped Piers to carry Sir Toby up to bed the night before. Then there was the old nurse, Mother Benson, expected back from her daughter's home in Tilbury next week. Jennet, a plaintive little creature of no more than thirteen years, acted as both kitchen maid and Rebecca's chambermaid, it seemed, for she was complaining bitterly to Mrs. Platt that she could do nothing right for Miss Rebecca today, and her ears were much the sorer for it.

"You thank your lucky stars, my girl," replied Mrs. Platt, "that you have a warm bed and a full belly. There's many a girl would give her eye teeth to be in the position you are."

Lucy looked across at the vacant-eyed, adenoidal child. Poor Jennet! She was not pretty, nor lively, in fact rather unprepossessing, and it was little wonder if a quick-tempered mistress continually found fault with her.

Not only did Lucy learn about the kitchen folk of the house, but through them she learnt about the family. Evidently Thomas and Piers were well-liked and respected, but for Elizabeth they seemed to have love and concern although she was so newly come to London.

"Poor bairn!" said Mrs. Platt. "I fancy she enjoys helping me in the kitchen sometimes – it puts her in mind of her mother and home. She's too young in her ways to be away from her mother, poor lamb."

"She's older than me," protested Jennet.

"Aye, but not half so wise in the ways of the world," retorted Mrs. Platt. "She's too gentle by half for city life; why, she even asks may she have her shoes cleaned or her gown pressed. I've never heard her give an order yet."

"Not so Madam Rebecca though, eh Jennet?" chuckled old Carew, the porter. "She keeps you running about."

Jennet groaned and got up to clear the dishes away. Lucy helped her wash and dry them, and stack them away. She had never seen so many dishes and platters, mugs and porringers in her life.

"Go down to the cellar and fetch up more coal, Carew," said Mrs. Platt then, "and Lucy, blow up the fire – you'll find the bellows in the corner. Mistress Rebecca and Lady Elizabeth will both be asking for hot water soon for their baths, then there's the warming pans to be put in the beds."

The mention of baths reminded Lucy of last night, and her first bath of her life. As she pumped the bellows vigorously, she wondered how often it was expected of one to take a bath.

"The ladies bath about once a month, but they're fanatic about cleanliness," Mrs. Platt told her. "The rest of us – well, it varies. Possibly about every six month, I should say." Jennet giggled.

"I 'aven't 'ad one this twelve month," she said.

"Right, then into Miss Rebecca's water you go – after she's finished," said Mrs. Platt firmly, and by the look on Jennet's face, Lucy concluded she wished she hadn't opened her mouth.

The morning dawned bright and clear. As Lucy stretched, savouring the comfort of a flock mattress and a truckle bed, with cotton sheets and warm woollen blankets the door opened softly and Elizabeth slipped in.

"Up Lucy, come, there is much to do today," she said, eager and anxious to begin. "First, the dressmaker. She already has the bolts of cloth Thomas allowed me to choose from his warehouse last week, so now we have to choose the designs. Come, we'll breakfast in my solar together, before the rest of the family are awake."

Mrs. Platt was already at work, lighting the fire and putting the cauldron on to boil. "Just some bread and cheese and some ale, if you please," Elizabeth said, and sat on a stool next to Lucy while they ate.

"Would you like milk?" Mrs. Platt asked. "Some asses' milk has just been delivered to the door."

"This is strange milk," said Lucy, "far thicker and creamier than that I am accustomed to."

"Asses' milk," explained Mrs. Platt. "None of your cow's milk here, that's watered down before it reaches the city, then again by the street sellers. No, asses, milked right here on your doorstep, into your own bowl, that's the only milk worth having."

As soon as they had eaten, Lucy and Elizabeth donned cloaks and set off to the dressmaker's. Lucy was amazed at the quantities of beautiful silks and satins, worsteds and woollens the dressmaker brought out and unrolled for Elizabeth to inspect and finger. Then they pored together over the minute dressed mannikins, and Elizabeth asked Lucy whether she preferred this design or that. By the time patterns and materials were agreed upon, and both Elizabeth's and Lucy's measurements taken, the sun was already high in the sky.

"Be sure to deliver the blue gown you are making for me by Friday, I pray you, Mistress Buckley, for I am to wear it to Court." Elizabeth smiled at the woman, and Lucy knew she had unwittingly guaranteed the arrival of the gown by Thursday. She had such a winning, pleasant way with her that all who met her could not fail to respond to her warmth.

"Once we are abroad, Lucy, I plan to take you with me everywhere. You shall be my companion, my friend, rather than my maid, I think," said Elizabeth as they walked along the sunlit street, pausing to look at the displays of pottery and pipes, clocks and guns on the shop stalls.

Lucy laughed, her deep-throated chuckle making Elizabeth smile. "You will be hard put to it to pass me off as a lady, I'm thinking! I have none of the accomplishments you have!"

"I don't know," said Elizabeth thoughtfully. "I do not need to teach you how to walk, for you have a natural grace already. As to speech, well, you may have to soften your tone just a little. And the other things are only surface things – painting, embroidery, playing the virginals – no one will call on you to do any of those. I think you could be a passably fair young lady if you put your mind to it. Do you read?"

"Yes," Lucy replied. "An old bookseller in the street taught me to ready and write and how to speak nicely."

Lucy laughed again. "You know, once I used to cherish a dream of becoming an actress. I used to loiter about at the entrance of the Globe theatre, in the vain hope I could attract the stage manager's attention. I would practise when I was alone, walking with little mincing steps and putting on a refined voice – here, I'll show you!"

She stopped short in the street and, making sure no-one was in sight, she struck an arrogant pose and began peeling off imaginary gloves. "Ho, there! Landlord! Fetch me a cup of sack and send the maid to warm me the best bed you have!" she drawled in an exaggerated, languid voice. "And be quick about it! I have travelled many a league this day."

Elizabeth was enthralled. "That's marvellous, Lucy, though a trifle overdone. Where did you learn this manner?"

"From the travellers – gentlemen usually – who came to stay at the Tabard. I imagined all wealthy people were born to speak with this air of authority." Piers certainly does, she thought inwardly, then wondered why she should think of him as an example.

Elizabeth walked for some time in silence, deep in thought. Suddenly inspiration struck. "Let us practise for a week, then one afternoon we shall go to walk in St. James' Park. Mayhap we shall meet there some of the acquaintances I have made in London. You shall go as my friend, and we shall see if you can pass yourself off as a lady."

She laughed happily at the prospect. Lucy was not so sure it was a good idea, but once having seized the notion, Elizabeth was not to be deterred.

Day after day she trained Lucy patiently, teaching her how to curtsey elegantly in the court fashion, and the intricacies of the steps of the Branles and the Corante, the fashionable dances His Majesty had introduced to the country. She taught her also how to carry a fan, and how to use it to convey the language of coquetry. Lucy was quick and willing to learn, and in no time she had mastered these arts.

"We really must do something now about your table manners," said Elizabeth one evening as they sat at supper. "You must learn to sip your wine elegantly – like this – and not throw it back like a man at his ale pot. And I know it is a little confusing to know which fork to use – let me help you sort them out." Mrs. Platt either was not interested as she served them their food, or was too busy with her mind on other matters to notice, but Rebecca snorted derisively when she came across the two girls dancing and flaunting their fans in the library one day.

"What use are fine manners to a tavern wench?" she muttered angrily. "Utter waste of time!", and with an annoyed click of the tongue she swept out.

Elizabeth smiled. "Pay no heed to her," she said. "You are doing well." And so the week passed.

Then one fine spring afternoon, dressed in the green gown and plush-lined cloak Elizabeth had given her, Lucy set off in the coach with Elizabeth. At the entrance to St. James' Park, Elizabeth dismissed the coach, ordering Carew to return for them in an hour.

Lucy's heart was beating fast with excitement. Ladies and gentlemen were sauntering everywhere in the warm sunshine, chatting and laughing as they walked along the Mall. To Lucy's eyes it was like fairyland, with the young elm and lime trees standing like sentinels at regular intervals along the Mall, and green meadows stretching either side, to the waters of the canal in the distance, where wild fowl wheeled and dipped. Beyond the trees she could see no sign of the sprawling city except the grey towers of the old Abbey against the skyline.

"Isn't it beautiful here?" enthused Elizabeth. "Thomas tells me the King has built ice-houses here in the Park, to keep his food and wines chilled all summer long. And he's just finished a deer enclosure too, I understand. 'T is no wonder this is said to be a favourite haunt of the King's," she said, gazing round her, enraptured. "Let us sit here a while on this bench and watch the people pass."

Lucy was no less fascinated by the scene than Elizabeth, by the ladies with their beautiful gowns revealing ornate petticoats, the fine lace, the fops with their over-large wigs and dandified speech, and the gentlemen walking their dogs or taking their children for a stroll. As she watched the elegant figures of two gentlemen approaching, Elizabeth suddenly nudged her and whispered in excitement, "Lucy look! It's Toby – with his friend, Lord James Baddeley! I wonder – Piers said Toby had no recollection of that night they went to the Tabard. Say not a word, Lucy, leave it to me."

Toby sauntered along, deep in conversation with his friend. A sudden flash of recognition lit up his eyes as he drew near the girls.

"Lady Elizabeth," he said graciously, "how delightful to meet you here. You already know James, I believe?"

Elizabeth bowed her head in recognition and smiled. Lord James bowed. Toby then transferred his gaze to Lucy, and a brief look of puzzlement crossed his eyes. He addressed Elizabeth again.

"Pray introduce us to your charming friend," he said. "I feel we must have met, but I cannot for the life of me remember when. No, we cannot have met, for such beauty would not lightly be forgotten," he said, not taking his eyes from Lucy's face. Lucy kept silent as Elizabeth had bidden her.

"Forgive me," said Elizabeth brightly and turned to Lucy. "May I introduce Sir Toby, Lord James – Mademoiselle Lucille, my friend." Quickly she turned again to Toby. "I regret Mademoiselle Lucille does not speak English."

"Indeed?" said Toby sounding more intrigued than ever. "May James and I offer you both some refreshments – some coffee, perhaps, or a snack?"

"Thank you, no," said Elizabeth. "I'm afraid we are late already. We must go. Goodbye, gentlemen."

She rose and turned to Lucy. "Viens, il nous faut rentrer," she said, holding out her hand so that Lucy could not fail to take her meaning.

As they walked away along the Mall, Lucy was aware of Toby's admiring looks following her, but she felt distinctly uncomfortable. Elizabeth was delighted with Toby's reaction to Lucy's masquerade. Admiration, Lucy decided, was not unpleasant, but how would Piers react if he came to know how she had deceived his friend? Her pleasure in the success of the afternoon, in being taking for a lady, was tempered with uneasy trepidation.

CHAPTER 5

Piers and Thomas were together in the study when Elizabeth and Lucy returned to Kempston House.

"I know only that Carew says he put her and her maid down at St. James' Park," Piers was saying to Thomas as they entered.

"Thank heaven you're here!" Thomas's face lost its anxious look and he hurried forward to meet Elizabeth with a smile. "I was a little worried about you, my dear, knowing your gentle, retiring nature, and that our parks are full of designing, predatory young men."

"Lucy was with me, Thomas, there was no danger." Elizabeth smiled disarmingly at him.

"Yes, a good watch-dog, I should think," commented Piers wryly. "That young lady seems quite capable of taking care of herself."

Lucy lowered her eyelids and wondered

what Piers would say if he discovered the trick played on Toby. He had considered her capable of theft; would he now think she had some base motive for this trick? Plotting to ensnare Toby, perhaps, after a rich husband for herself? Oh no!

Elizabeth was talking animatedly. "It's the most beautiful material, Thomas, I am grateful to you. And Mistress Buckley is to deliver the gown in good time for my presentation on Friday, so all is now in hand."

"You have gloves, stockings?" asked Thomas.

"I shall go to the haberdasher's with Lucy in the morning," replied Elizabeth. At the mention of Lucy's name, Piers turned and saw Lucy was still standing inside the door.

"Have you no work to do, Lucy?" he asked. "You have much to learn as a lady's maid. Maids do not usually listen to family conversations."

Lucy flushed angrily, and was about to retort as she would have done at the Tabard, then checked herself. He was only trying to teach her how a maid should behave.

"I'm sorry. I did not intend ... I shall go," she said. Elizabeth turned to her. "Thank you, Lucy, you have been most helpful today, I am grateful to you," she said. "Please take my cloak."

As Lucy left the room she heard Elizabeth say brightly, "By the way, Piers, I met that charming but irresponsible Sir Toby in the Park today." Lucy wondered, as she closed the door behind her, whether Elizabeth was going to reveal their prank. If she did, Lucy felt sure she would soon hear from Piers.

Rebecca pushed past her into the study. "Out of my way, girl," she said impatiently. Lucy remembered Elizabeth had implied that she and Rebecca did not get along well together. No wonder, thought Lucy, she had a thoroughly disagreeable manner.

Later that evening Lucy sat alone, waiting for the smoothing iron to heat at the fire so as to press Elizabeth's cloak. Suddenly she heard a step and looked up.

"You look very pensive," said Piers in his rich, vibrant voice. "Whenever I have seen you before you have been fiery and tetchy. This is a pleasant change."

What did he mean, she wondered. Was he being ironic? Oh, why should she concern herself about his opinion of her? It was Thomas, her employer, and Elizabeth whose opinion mattered, surely?

"What, no quick repartee?" he said, with

an amused smile.

"Do you wish something of me, Master Piers?" she said dutifully, remembering how he had taught her her place.

"Only to say that Elizabeth has told us of the trick you played on Sir Toby."

She turned on him, her resolution forgotten. "And will you now rebuke me for that?" She stood erect, stiff, ready for battle.

"Hold, hold! You are a fiery maid in truth! A temper to match your hair, it would seem! No, I would not reproach you, Lucy, Elizabeth said it was her idea. Sir Toby's antics make him fair game to have a trick played on him now and again. No harm has been done and I find the affair rather amusing. I came only to repeat what I said, that I believe you to be a girl capable of taking good care of herself and that as the Lady Elizabeth is far more gently nurtured and open to deception, I would beg a favour of you."

Lucy was surprised and extremely pleased. That a man so authoritative as Piers should beg a favour of her, was flattery indeed. "If I can, sir," she replied.

"You can, Lucy, be assured you can," he said gravely. "I would ask you while you are abroad to look out for Lady Elizabeth, as for yourself. To protect her against evils she does not yet know exist. I know you understand me, Lucy. Mother Benson is kind, but no longer capable."

Lucy did not ask him to explain. "There was no need to ask me this as a favour," she answered. "My devotion to Elizabeth is hers already. I would go through fire and water for her."

Piers smiled. It was remarkable, but Lucy had not noticed before what a singularly sweet smile he had. It completely altered the stern look he usually wore.

"Thank you," he said, putting a hand on her shoulder. "I know Thomas would be grateful to you too, but he also is an innocent as far as the world is concerned, except in matters of business."

At that moment Rebecca entered. She looked at Piers, who withdrew his hand from Lucy's shoulder. "I see you have the iron heated," she said to Lucy with an amused smile. "Press my gown for me, Lucy," and she tossed it to her casually. "Clumsy child," she added coldly as it fell through Lucy's grasp, then smiled warmly at Piers.

"Excuse me," said Piers and passing Rebecca, went out. Rebecca looked none too pleased, thought Lucy, as she bent to retrieve the gown.

"Bring me my gown when it is done, and take care you do it well," Rebecca said sharply and went to leave. At the doorway she paused and added, "Not content with Sir Toby, you coquette with my cousin, I see. Have a care, girl, or you'll find yourself back in the gutter whence you came."

With that, she disappeared through the door.

Yet again Lucy's anger rose inside her. Was she always to be misunderstood? Coquette with Piers? Shame flushed her cheeks at the very idea. And Rebecca's tone had been decidedly acid and unpleasant, triumphant even, when she threatened to throw Lucy out.

No wonder Elizabeth did not care for Rebecca's company, Lucy reflected. She was a thoroughly disagreeable person. It was only as Lucy ran the smoothing iron over Rebecca's gown that she remembered that Rebecca had a maid of her own, Jennet. Why hadn't Rebecca ordered Jennet to press her gown? Where was Jennet?

An hour passed. Lucy put away the iron and blew up the fire again, and finding there was no coal left in the box, she went down in the cellar to the coal hole. She shivered as she descended the dark steps, lifting her full skirts in one hand and holding a candle in the other. As she drew the bolt on the heavy door of the coal hole, she saw Jennet, filthy and tear-stained, sitting amid the coals.

"What in heaven's name...?" said Lucy in surprise. The child ran to her and clutched at his skirts.

"Miss Rebecca locked me in here this afternoon," she whimpered.

"Why?"

"She said I pulled her hair as I was combing it." Jennet was still sobbing as they climbed the stairs again.

This time it was not only anger but hatred too that rose unbidden in Lucy. She hated to see any poor, defenceless thing attacked, and this poor clumsy creature was rendered even more clumsy and frightened by her mistress's continual harassing. And then to punish the frightened little creature by locking her in the dark cellar, alone, for hours on end, and to forget her existence – this to Lucy was criminal.

She was burning with indignation when she went up to Rebecca's room to return the gown. What could she do or say, she who was only a servant in the house as Piers had already reminded her? To say anything would probably only invite further malice, directed both at Jennet and herself, since Rebecca had accused her of trying to capture Piers' fancy.

Rebecca was not in her room. Lucy lay the gown on the bed and withdrew. Still white with anger, she took Elizabeth's cloak to her.

"What is troubling you, Lucy? Is something wrong?" said Elizabeth, full of concern when she saw Lucy's tight-lipped face.

Lucy told her of Rebecca's accusation, which Elizabeth found amusing, and then of Jennet's imprisonment for the whole afternoon and evening. Elizabeth was shocked.

"You did not say anything to reproach Rebecca, I hope. Even Thomas would not deem that fitting. I shall speak to her. It is my duty, as mistress of Kempston House," she said quietly, but Lucy could see by her expression that it was not a prospect she relished. "It will not be easy, for Rebecca has been mistress here since she was orphaned. She was brought up here, and I think a little spoiled."

"Oh no, Elizabeth. Do not involve yourself in any disagreement with your family on my behalf. After all, we shall be leaving

Kempston House shortly," Lucy pleaded. She did not like to think she was responsible for any ill-feeling in the family, on account of her own sudden bursts of anger.

"You are right, Lucy. We would not wish to leave here with an unpleasant atmosphere. I shall try to make some recompense to Jennet – Rebecca need not know. No, that is deceitful. I know – I shall ask Thomas his opinion. He will think of some happier solution," Elizabeth's face brightened.

Lucy was touched by her faith in Thomas. Even if Elizabeth did not love her husband, she did respect and admire him. Maybe in Elizabeth's eyes he replaced the father she had loved and lost not long ago. The feeling that now stirred in Lucy seemed remarkably like envy, but she thrust it out of her mind as unworthy of her. Maybe she did not have someone to lean upon and respect as Elizabeth had, but she had been endowed with an independent, strong-willed nature to compensate for it. She was strong enough to take care of herself – Piers had said so.

Piers – why did everything she thought about relate to Piers? Why should he disturb her so? Possibly because she was always uncertain how she stood with him. One minute he was reminding her she was a servant, and the next he was treating her as an equal, begging a favour of her. Of only one thing was she sure; they had their concern for Elizabeth's welfare in common.

The trip abroad with Elizabeth would bring one boon with it, at least, she reflected. It would put a great distance between her and that malicious Rebecca, and Piers would no longer be there to disturb her. In the meantime there were other matters to occupy her mind. On Friday Elizabeth was to be presented at Court, and Lucy determined that nothing untoward must happen to spoil Elizabeth's great day. That was the day, as it turned out, that Thomas had to leave for York. Elizabeth was sad, but the prospect of the evening excited her.

She was to be presented by Lady Estelle Devereux, a childhood friend of her mother's. The evening came at last, and Elizabeth, excited and happy, put on the gentian blue gown the dressmaker had delivered, over a petticoat trimmed with silver lace. She looked very lovely, Lucy thought, her cheeks tinged with a glow of excitement and her glossy fair hair hanging in ringlets and looped with silver ribbons.

"Now you, Lucy," said Elizabeth, happily. "Put on your apple green gown quickly, for we must hurry. Lady Devereux will be here presently."

Lady Devereux was tall and elegant; though she was now plump and no longer young, her face still showed that she had been quite a beauty twenty years earlier. She greeted Elizabeth tenderly and asked after her mother, whom she had not seen for several years, then led the way to the waiting coach.

Soon they arrived at Whitehall, where the King entertained every day, Lady Devereux told them.

"Shall we see the Queen too?" asked Elizabeth.

Lady Devereux looked at Elizabeth. "That's highly unlikely," she said. "The Queen only comes to Whitehall for state occasions. Although she has a bedchamber here, usually she stays at Somerset House." She stopped as she saw Elizabeth's wide-eyed look of innocence. "Do you hear naught of Court gossip in Northumberland?" she asked Elizabeth.

"Very little," Elizabeth admitted.

Lady Devereux looked from Elizabeth to Lucy and said, "I see I shall have to enlighten you, but not at the moment."

As Lucy and Lady Devereux helped

Elizabeth to arrange her dress and hair in an ante-room, Lucy pondered over Lady Devereux's words. As a native of London Lucy had heard the King led a very merry life and that he was reputed to have a least one mistress, but of Queen Catherine she knew little. She did remember seeing her once, three years ago, when the King had brought his new bride from Hampton Court to London by barge, but all Lucy could see of her from the bank was that she was dark-skinned and so were her ladies-in-waiting. According to gossip, Queen Catherine was a much-neglected wife now.

Lady Devereux led Elizabeth away and Lucy was left to her own devices. She grew impatient with the wearisome chatter of the other maids, and left the ante-room. The great gallery was thronged with people, ladies and gentlemen elegantly dressed, maids and servants, pageboys and liveried footmen. Lucy joined the crowd, certain that no-one in this enormous crowd would realise she was only a lady's maid. She was anxious to see more of life in Whitehall Palace.

The gallery was ornate and very magnificent. She saw elegantly dressed men with ladies on their laps, chatting and laughing, flirting and caressing. She saw a group of men around a table, and on drawing closer, she saw they were playing cards. In the centre of the table lay a mountain of golden guineas. One of the players, a fairhaired handsome youth, was trying to shake off a maid of honour whose arm was around his neck.

"Come, enough of your game of basset," she was saying. "There are other sports to be enjoyed." Lucy watched her as she turned the man's head towards her, thrusting her full white bosom in its low-cut gown under his face, and pulling him gently with voluptuous movements.

"Enough of your pertness, madam, I am not of a humour to romp with you tonight," he answered peevishly.

"Have done, then, I'll find another more tractable than you," she snapped angrily, and turned away.

Lucy smiled inwardly. Ladies and gentlemen, it would seem, were no different from maids and menservants, and what was happening here in Whitehall could equally well have been taking place in the Tabard.

"Il y a quelquechose d'amusant?" she heard a voice say. She turned and found herself face to face with Sir Toby. By the flush on his cheeks and the gleam in his eyes, she guessed he had been quaffing liberal quantities of wine once again.

"Mademoiselle Lucille, n'est-ce pas? Je suis vraiment heureux de vous revoir, mademoiselle," he said, smiling broadly.

What in heaven's name was he saying? Whatever it was, he must still be under the impression that she was a French lady, as Elizabeth had told him. What was she to do? To tell him she was only Lucy, a maid, would be to brand Elizabeth a liar. She decided to say nothing, and continued to watch the card-players.

"Oho," muttered Toby, "a frosty French maid, are you not? Or is it only shyness, I wonder? Come, let us dance. We have your French dances here at Court, mademoiselle, so you should feel truly at home."

Without more ado he took her firmly by the hand and pulled her after him. But as he led her into the ballroom, the music stopped. A tall, dark-browed man with a gentle, melancholy look in his eye clapped his hands and announced, "And now Michel, our little page, shall sing, and Signor Corbetta shall accompany him on the guitar. Francesco, begin."

Toby groaned. "Once he starts Corbetta

playing and that boy singing, he will not let them cease. I think His Majesty prefers music and love to dancing."

His Majesty! Then this was the King, Charles, the Black Boy, as he was nick-named, this man in velvet and point lace, sitting on a chair, entranced by the music. Lucy could hardly believe it. At this close range she could see clearly his dark, sombre eyes and his long, unusually long, straight nose and heavy underlip. She stood watching him, fascinated by the thought that this was the man who neglected his gentle wife and captivated all the women who met him, or so people said.

Toby's hand gripped her arm. "Come, my lovely, another drink and then a kiss, I think. You are a shy and lovely creature, Lucille, and thank heaven you do not speak English. Your pretty cheeks would blush with shame if you knew what I would wish. I shall teach you the pleasures of Court life. Come!"

His voice was slurred and still there was that dull gleam in his eyes. She knew only too well what he wished, Lucy thought to herself. Suddenly he grabbed her as he had done once before.

"What's sauce for the King is sauce for the courtier," he announced solemnly, and kissed her, hard and long. No-one noticed or commented, for so many other couples there in Whitehall were engaged in the same pursuit. Or so Lucy thought, until a voice she knew only too well said icily, "Where is the Lady Elizabeth? I have come to escort her home." It was Piers.

CHAPTER 6

On the homeward journey in the coach there was an oppressive air of silence. Lucy was sitting next to Piers, who sat stiff and unsmiling, and opposite her Elizabeth seemed very subdued. Only Lady Devereux broke the silence from time to time to exclaim irritably when the coach lurched and bumped over the potholes in the road.

Lucy was apprehensive. What must Piers be thinking of her now, having found her in Toby's embrace? She stole a sideways glance at him and saw he was frowning and his lips were set in a hard line.

At Kempston House Piers helped Elizabeth and Lucy to alight, then drove off again to escort Lady Devereux home.

In her bedchamber, Elizabeth let Lucy help her disrobe in silence. Lucy wondered what ailed her.

"You look sad, Elizabeth. Did you not enjoy your visit to Whitehall?" she asked her at length. Elizabeth turned her huge, sad eyes to her.

"Oh Lucy! I had heard that Court life was gay since Charles was King, but never that it was so depraved. What I saw with my own eyes shocked me utterly, but what Lady Devereux told me – of the King, of his poor neglected Queen, and his mistresses! Yes, mistresses – several of them! That made my heart sad. And Lady Devereux talked of it all as if it was something enjoyable – she talked in a scandalised tone, of course, but she seemed to regard it as rather amusing. Oh Lucy! If this is London court life, it is not for me! I would I were home again in Northumberland!"

"What was it shocked you?" Lucy asked gently.

"The drinking, the gambling for huge stakes – I saw one man lose his house, horse, carriage, all he possessed. And the public lovemaking! Oh Lucy! Have they no shame?"

"Did you find nothing to please you, then?" Lucy urged, anxious to dispel Elizabeth's gloom.

"Well yes, I did enjoy the dancing, and I met the King and I thought him so charm-ing, before Lady Devereux told me all those things about him. He had such a melancholy look in his dark eyes, and he was so witty. He was sitting chatting to me, with one of his dogs on his lap – he loves spaniels you know, Lucy. Lady Devereux told me so – in fact, she said, he's so fond of his dogs he allows them to sleep and even to have their litters in his bedchamber. The result is, she says, the chamber smells dreadfully."

Lucy laughed, partly at the idea of the King having a bed-chamber that smelt, and partly to put Elizabeth in good humour again. She was gratified to see Elizabeth's face relax a little, losing some of its worried tension.

"Let me tell you what happened to me, then," Lucy said, and went on to relate as humorously as she could the subterfuge with Sir Toby. "It's as well His Majesty stopped the dancing when he did," she chuckled, "or Sir Toby would perforce have discovered I was no lady, French or English, I was so nervous, I'd have trampled his feet!"

Elizabeth laughed. "I have already taught you the Branles and the Corante, Lucy, and I learnt a new French dance tonight that the King has introduced to Court. Tomorrow we shall practise it together." She was happy again now, with something to look forward to. Lucy was glad.

Piers was in the vestibule, taking off his cloak when Lucy went downstairs. He still wore a serious, thoughtful look, and Lucy mentally braced herself for what he would say about Toby and herself.

"Lucy, a moment," he said quietly. She approached him and stood silent before him. "Can you have Lady Elizabeth's luggage ready and packed by Monday morning? I think it were best we leave London somewhat earlier than we planned. We shall take the Dover coach from the Swan at dawn on Monday."

Lucy was taken by surprise. Surely he was not removing her and Elizabeth from London earlier than planned just because of Toby? There was but one way to find out.

"Have you spoken to Sir Toby, sir?" she asked him.

Piers looked surprised. "Toby? Well, yes, I did have a few words with him this evening. I gathered you and Elizabeth are still hoodwinking my friend; he was still under the impression you were a visitor from France, a Mademoiselle Lucille, he said, but I quickly disillusioned him on that score. Why do you ask?"

"Was he very angry?" asked Lucy, ignoring his question.

"Why no, in fact he was rather amused. But I do not understand the import of your question. Why do you ask of Toby?"

"He is the reason we leave London on Monday, is he not?"

Piers laughed, a short, humourless laugh. "No, by my faith. Tho' I must admit your behaviour gives one good reason to doubt your virtue." Lucy's face burned as he went on. "I would it were such a trivial reason." He looked at her for a moment. "I shall tell you, Lucy, but I would ask you not to repeat what I say to Lady Elizabeth for fear of worrying her. As you may know, there have been several cases of plague in London during the past week, and now the number of cases doubles almost daily. Today there are two houses in the next street to us with the red cross marked on the door, and the words, 'The Lord have mercy on us' writ large upon them."

Lucy forgot her anger. She understood his apprehension. It had happened before that a plague epidemic ran unchecked though the city, though not for many years now. From what Piers said, it would seem another might be beginning.

"With luck, perchance the coming winter will check it before it gets a strong grip on the city," he went on, "but it were best Elizabeth left here as soon as possible. She seems to be none too strong a creature. But mark what I say, Lucy, not a word to Elizabeth."

In the succeeding two days Lucy managed to prepare and pack, with Elizabeth's help, giving her to understand that they were to depart early so as to take their time to Dover.

Piers sent word to Mother Benson to return at once to Kempston House. The messenger returned to say Mother Benson was ill and unable to be moved, her daughter said. Lucy and Piers exchanged swift significant glances.

"Then Elizabeth and I will have to travel alone," said Lucy.

"Have no fear, I shall see you aboard ship and then Monsieur Garenne is to meet you at Calais," Piers replied.

Lucy could guess from his eyes the unspoken fear. Elizabeth's removal from danger was imperative.

In the chill grey dawn on Monday Piers helped them into the coach. Rebecca watched silently from the doorstep. Elizabeth leaned out of the coach and waved as Carew drove off. Piers sat opposite Lucy, and she saw he still had the abstracted air of a man whose mind was on other matters.

As the coach clattered across London Bridge, a drizzling rain began to fall. By the time they reached the Swan Inn, where the Dover coach was to leave from, it was falling heavily. Lucy led Elizabeth into the inn while Piers supervised the loading of their portmanteaux and hair trunks on to the Dover coach. Rain was beating on the inn windows, and the tall candles guttered in their sockets. Elizabeth sat pale and silent, her fair hair falling about her shoulders when she threw back her hood. She did truly look fragile and vulnerable, thought Lucy, and she was glad Elizabeth was not to remain in London.

Finally, the coach left, the coachman huddled deep into the folds of his coat against the driving rain. The clatter and rumble of the wheels over London's paved streets soon gave way to a lurching roll when they reached the unpaved muddy roads leading towards Kent.

Gradually it grew lighter as they bumped uncomfortably through Dartford to Gravesend. Here they stopped for a meal, then journeyed on to Rochester, where they were to stay the night. Lucy noticed that Elizabeth had barely touched the roast beef, and was growing visibly paler at every jolt.

"Thank heaven we can rest here the night," Elizabeth said as they got down at the Red Lion in Rochester. "I do not think I could have travelled another mile."

Lucy saw her to the room Piers had ordered for her, and Elizabeth lay down and fell soundly asleep. Once again Lucy was struck by her fragile, ethereal look, and her heart warmed with protective love for her.

Next dawn they were on the road again, Elizabeth smiling wanly, but looking happier than the previous night. The rain had lessened in severity, but still the countryside was cloaked in a mist of drizzle. Piers' air of constraint had gradually fallen away as they put more miles between them and London, and by the time they reached Dover at nightfall he was his usual self, abrupt but friendly.

As they stepped down from the coach Lucy smelt the salty tang of the sea. Her senses quickened and a swift thrill of excitement ran through her. Up to now, the journey had been merely a subject for discussion, but now she began to experience the real thrill of anticipation.

The feeling was heightened when Piers took them aboard the packet boat, 'The Adventurer'. Lucy, on deck, saw him speak quietly to the ship's captain, and put money in his hand. As he neared the gangplank to descend, he came face to face with her.

"Everything is arranged, Lucy. You will be met at Calais by Monsieur Garenne. May God speed you both," he said quietly.

"What shall you do, Master Piers?" Lucy asked him. "You will surely not stay in London?"

"I must," he answered. "But perchance I shall be in Paris – on business, you understand – before very long, and I shall take the opportunity of visiting you then."

He stopped speaking and looked along the quay for a moment. Then he turned again to Lucy. "Lucy, I asked you once to do a favour for me. Would you repeat the kindness and do me yet another?"

"But of course, sir – if I can," Lucy replied.

"Then take this letter," he said, producing an envelope from the folds of his cloak. "Deliver it in person, and for the love of God, tell no-one your errand. Will you do this for me? I must warn you, though, that discovery could bring you into great danger. I would deliver it myself, but in the circumstances I cannot leave Rebecca alone in London for so long."

Lucy's eyes shone. Piers was entrusting something he obviously valued – to her!

"I cannot tell you of the significance of this letter," he went on, "but it is of the utmost importance that it reaches its destination safely. Are you willing to take the risk?"

"Yes," Lucy answered firmly. Whatever the letter contained, Lucy was convinced of one thing. Piers would do nothing that was dishonourable, nor ask her to do so. And it must be something of very great importance.

"I am eternally grateful to you." His sigh of relief was almost audible. He put his arm round Lucy's shoulders and led her towards the gangplank. At the step he turned to her.

"As soon as you are able, deliver it to the baker in the Rue Flambeau. Say nothing of how you got it, and tell no-one of your mission. I am entrusting the letter and my sister-in-law to you, and I know you will protect both with your life if necessary. I could not put either in better hands," he said solemnly, then he turned and was gone.

CHAPTER 7

Lucy felt very happy that night as she settled down in a cramped bunk in the master's cabin with Elizabeth. Now she knew Piers trusted and respected her.

When the tide turned, 'The Adventurer' set sail for France. To Lucy's relief the crossing was smooth for the time of year and Elizabeth suffered no ill effects. Disembarking at Calais was a hectic affair, with passes to be signed, and luggage items to be paid for and ferried ashore, but as Elizabeth's French was fluent, and her charm so apparent, they were soon safely ashore.

There they were met by Monsieur Garenne, a merchant acquaintance of Thomas's who had agreed to rent a small house and hire house-servants for Elizabeth's use and to keep a kindly eye on her in Paris.

In the succeeding days as Lucy and Elizabeth settled in the Rue d'Avignon, Lucy felt a sense of elation whenever she touched the letter in her pocket. Once again it reminded her of Piers' trust in her. Tell no-one, he had said, so Lucy dare not tell even Elizabeth of her errand. As soon as she could, she must find the Rue Flambeau alone.

"Now we are away from home with no-one to keep surveillance over us, you are no longer Lucy Howe, chambermaid, but my friend, Miss Lucy Howe, lady," Elizabeth said one morning over breakfast. "You shall accompany me to Madame Garenne's this evening, for she has invited us to a soirée to meet some of her friends. I know what you are about to say," she said, waving aside Lucy's protests, "that you do not speak the language, but to meet people and make an effort to communicate is the best possible way to learn."

She smiled sympathetically. "Do not worry, Lucy, you are a born mimic and very quick to learn, as I have already discovered. And I shall try to teach you."

By the time that evening's soirée was at an end, Lucy felt exhausted after her efforts to communicate. More gesticulation than words had been necessary, but she had picked up a few basic phrases. Her education had begun in earnest.

"Madame Garenne found you quite entrancing, my dear," Elizabeth told her joyfully, "and her friends are only too anxious to invite us to their homes. I am so happy for you, Lucy, but for myself, I do not wish to lead such a gay social life. I would be far happier if I could be left to enjoy these books and virginals and do my embroidery and painting." She waved to indicate the book-lined walls of the room, and her painting materials laid out on a side table. "Piers thinks I have some talent, and should foster it by practice," she added shyly.

The mention of Piers' name jolted Lucy's conscience. His letter still lay, undelivered, hidden amongst her clothing in the press upstairs. He had said to deliver it as soon as possible and they had been in Paris almost a week already, and she had still not discovered where the Rue Flambeau lay.

Her chance arrived when she found Elizabeth poring over a map of Paris.

"We are not far from the Bois de Boulogne, Lucy. We must go and ride on horseback there. It's rather like our own Hyde Park, I understand from Piers. I expect he will be here before long, to settle matters with Monsieur Garenne, who is in charge of the money matters pertaining to our visit. Thomas did not want me to risk travelling with a large sum of money."

So that was why Piers had said he would be in Paris soon, Lucy reflected. Then what was the letter about? And to whom? She pushed it out of her mind. It was none of her business. Only the mission to deliver it was her affair.

Over Elizabeth's shoulder she scanned the map of Paris. Elizabeth traced out with her finger the route to the Bois, and Lucy was able to see the Rue Flambeau, some two miles away from the house.

"I shall teach you how to mount a horse when the ostler cups his hands for you, and how to sit side-saddle," said Elizabeth. "And then you will be prepared for when we hire horses from the livery stables."

Lucy's mind was not on horses but on how to get to the baker in the Rue Flambeau. In the next few days she practised speaking French with Jeanne, the little maid-of-all-work who cooked for them, until she felt confident she could move around Paris without getting lost. Now was the time, she thought, to suggest to Elizabeth that she, Lucy, should go out and do some of their shopping for provisions, and on the way, perhaps she could manage to reach the baker.

Before she could broach the subject, Madame Garenne arrived in a great flurry of excitement. She poured out a long story to Elizabeth with voluble Gallic gestures and spoke so rapidly in her excitement that Lucy could make out only occasional words like le comte and le bal. Elizabeth nodded and replied quietly to her.

"Madame Garenne was very excited, was she not?" Lucy commented to Elizabeth after Jeanne had shown Madame Garenne out.

"Indeed, yes. It seems the Vicomtesse de Rathez has invited Madame Garenne to a ball this evening and asked her to bring her English friends too."

"That's wonderful!" said Lucy in delight. "Imagine a ball! What shall you wear, Elizabeth?"

"I shall not go," replied Elizabeth firmly. Lucy's face fell. "But you shall. You have already captured the hearts of Madame Garenne's friends. You shall go in my place, Lucy. You like fun and excitement and meeting people, and I would much prefer to remain at home."

And despite all Lucy's protests Elizabeth was adamant that Lucy was to go alone. Madame Garenne was disappointed at

Elizabeth's absence but delighted that Lucy was to come.

She introduced her to the Vicomtesse, who in turn took Lucy on a tour of all her guests. The ladies were charmed by her and the men too were attentive. Lucy did the tour of one bejewelled lady to the next, and finally, overcome by voluble French chatter, she went to stand alone in a corner.

"You are the English lady, are you not?" Lucy looked up into a pair of piercing blue eyes.

"Allow me to introduce myself, Count Reichendorf, like yourself a visitor to this country," the gentleman said. "At your service, Fräulein." He bowed, slightly. "May I fetch you some wine?" He continued to gaze hard at her with that penetrating look as he led her to a brocade-covered settee where they sat and talked a while of their impressions of Paris, and Lucy noted how well he spoke English, apart from a somewhat guttural accent. It was rather attractive, she thought, as indeed was the Count himself, with his broad shoulders, blond hair and those keen blue eyes.

"Have you visited England, sir?" she asked him eventually.

"To be sure, Fräulein," he answered, "and

I found it a very lovely country. I particularly admired some of your buildings in London – the Banqueting Hall at Whitehall, for instance. I am very fond of good architecture. Have you been to Whitehall or St. James' when King Charles was entertaining?" he asked.

"I was at Whitehall of late," Lucy replied, "and in truth, I found it rather amusing."

She noticed how his eyes narrowed at that, but the Vicomtesse returned at that moment to bear Lucy away to meet another guest. Throughout the evening Lucy found the Count was hovering nearby, and when the time came to leave, he was still at her elbow.

"Allow me to see you to your coach, Fräulein," he said gravely. Lucy accepted his offer, and as he handed her into the coach he bowed and said, "I am delighted to have made your acquaintance, Lady Elizabeth, having heard so much about your beauty and charm, and I hope we shall meet again."

Before Lucy could open her mouth to point out that there must be some mistake, she was not the Lady Elizabeth, he had bowed and was gone.

Elizabeth thought it was rather amusing. "Well, why not?" she said. "If you can carry out social visits in my place, why not let him think you are Lady Elizabeth? There you are, I told you you could be convincing as a lady. And I shall be left in peace to paint and embroider as I prefer."

The following day Lucy thought her opportunity had come to deliver Piers' letter. Elizabeth was preoccupied with her painting, so she decided to slip out alone. With luck, none of her acquaintances would see her, for it was not considered safe for a lady to walk abroad alone.

With the letter tucked safely into the sleeve of her gown, she set off on foot towards the Rue Flambeau. It was bitterly cold and she was grateful to have the plush-lined cloak Elizabeth had given her, to wrap closely to her body.

She had memorised the way from the map, and had covered about half the distance when she was overtaken by a coach.

"Lady Elizabeth!" a voice cried, and an elegantly dressed man stepped down from the coach in front of her. It was the Count. "Gnädiges Fräulein!" he said, and there was concern in his voice. "Why are you walking the streets of the city alone, and on foot? You obviously have no conception of the risks you are running, walking abroad without at least a manservant. Please, allow me to conduct you wherever you wish to go," and graciously he helped her to climb into his coach.

"You are most kind, Count Reichendorf," Lucy smiled at him. "I was just going to purchase some water colours, and thought it would provide me with some exercise to walk and at the same time afford me an opportunity to see this fine city."

He seemed content with her answer. "But please, allow me to show you Paris," he urged, his keen gaze again making her look away. "The buildings here are very fine. I believe I told you of my deep interest in architecture; if you are an artist, possibly you too appreciate fine buildings?"

Lucy hesitated, then murmured an excuse that she was interested in architecture indeed, but had had little opportunity to visit any buildings of importance, living as she did, in virtual seclusion until recently.

"I shall take you to see the Notre Dame Cathedral," the Count announced gravely, "and then the Louvre. I am sure you will love the new Italian style, as I do. Your own Inigo Jones was much influenced by it. You will allow me, my lady, the pleasure of escorting you around Paris, will you not? I am sure we shall find we have much in common."

Lucy thanked him politely. After they had bought the paints, the Count drove her back to the Rue d'Avignon.

"With your permission, Fräulein, I shall call for you at ten in the morning and we shall begin with the Cathedral of Notre Dame," he said, bowed politely, and was gone.

Lucy went to Elizabeth's chamber and told her of the encounter.

"Do go with him, and learn all you can of Paris," Elizabeth urged. "Your education will be greater than mine by the time we return to England," she laughed. "By the way, Madame Garenne has called again today – there is to be another soirée tomorrow evening, so do not return too late from Notre Dame.

"I shall be busy with Jeanne in the kitchen. I intend to be a good wife to Thomas, so practised I am becoming in culinary skills and housekeeping," she remarked to Lucy, her face flushed with pride in her achievements. "And today there was a new woman, Casilde the laundress. She brought the most delightful baby with her. It was a real joy for me to be able to nurse him. This is a wonderful holiday for us both, is it not, Lucy, when we are both able to do what we truly enjoy?"

The letter lay still undelivered. Lucy's conscience began to gnaw. There was blossom on the trees already, and they put her in mind of the trees in bloom in London, and from there her thoughts strayed to Molly and Garth. If only they could see her present life! Would they not be surprised and happy to see her leading the life of a lady?

Lucy felt uneasy about Molly too. She had sent Molly no more money as she had planned, because she and Elizabeth had left London so quickly on account of the plague.

The plague! Lucy realised she had not given a thought to that since they had left London. Were Molly and Garth safe? And Piers and Thomas too? There had been several letters from Thomas in the past weeks, but only speaking of trade, Elizabeth said, nothing of London.

Lucy felt very uncomfortable about her selfish behaviour since coming to Paris. She resolved to deliver Piers' letter somehow, and quickly, getting rid of the Count by some means or other. She would also ask

Elizabeth to write to Thomas for news and to ask if he would send a small sum of money to Molly out of her wages.

Thus eased in her mind, Lucy fell fast asleep.

CHAPTER 8

The Count was bringing Lucy home from the Notre Dame.

"Tomorrow we shall ride in the Bois," he said. He never asked her, Lucy noticed, he simply dictated quietly what they were to do. "Did you enjoy this morning?" he continued.

"Why yes indeed," Lucy answered, smiling. Indeed she had. Flirtation and coquetry was as much expected of a lady here as it was in London, and he responded gallantly. Never before had Lucy felt so confident, so sure of her own attractions.

"I see," the Count murmured. He looked at his shoes for a moment, then looked up. "You enjoy the attention of many men, my lady?"

Lucy laughed, a little embarrassed. "But of course, every maid likes to think she is attractive to men," she said.

"You are very attractive, Fräulein," he said

gravely, and looked away out of the window. Lucy was surprised that the Count found her so; he had seemed always so serious, so intellectual. He remained silent for some moments, then seemed to make up his mind. He turned to her earnestly.

"Elizabeth," he said in a low, urgent voice, "you are without doubt the most fascinating woman I have ever met. Up to now women as a whole have held little attraction for me – empty-headed, feather-brained creatures, most of them. But your deep interest in matters other than clothes shows me you are above other women."

Lucy, who had sat thus far bewildered by the suddenness of his declaration, could barely repress a giggle. What would Count Reichendorf say if he knew he was declaring his feelings thus to a tavern maid? She was enjoying the game of flirtation she has mastered so well recently.

"Sir," she said with mock humility, lowering her eyes. "I'll wager you make this unusual approach to many ladies."

"Gott in Himmel!" he exclaimed in shocked tones. "Never! I swear Elizabeth, you are the first woman who has had the power to stir me!" He picked up her hand from her lap, and pressed it between his own. "You must believe me, Elizabeth. You are the only woman for me!" His blue eyes were wide and serious.

"But Count, you forget yourself. I am a married woman," protested Lucy. Since he still believed her to be Elizabeth, he must know Elizabeth was married.

"So I understand," he replied, "but I also understand, if I have not been misled, that though you are a wife in name, you will not be truly a wife to your husband until your return to England. If that is so, Elizabeth, it will be a small problem to have your marriage annulled. Then you would be free to marry me," he finished, with the satisfied air of a man who had thought all the problems out carefully and found all the right solutions.

Lucy did not reply. She was stunned at his coolness. He was in effect proposing marriage to her, without even saying he loved her.

The Count was still caressing her hand. "Tell me, Elizabeth, is it true?"

"Is what true?" she asked.

"That you are a virgin still? I must know – tell me – are you still a maid?"

Lucy looked at him. The keen eyes seemed to bore into her. She looked down at the floor, and slowly up at him again.

"I swear it – I am a maid – and shall remain so until I give myself to the man I love," she answered levelly.

His face relaxed. He pressed her hand again. "Then I would ask you to consider my proposal," he said.

"But I do not love you," Lucy replied.

"Not yet, my love, but there is time to learn," he said in a superior, fatherly way. "We are here, in the Rue d'Avignon. I shall call for you in the morning at ten for our ride."

"But sir," Lucy protested, seeing her chance, "you must give me time to consider what you have said. Please leave me time to think."

"How long?" he asked sharply.

"A few days – say, till the week's end?" she answered hopefully. If she could shake him off until then, there might at last be an opportunity to try again to reach the Rue Flambeau and the baker with Piers' letter.

"Very well," he agreed. "Until Friday then."

The coach clattered to a halt and the Count helped her alight, then bid her goodnight quickly and was gone.

Lucy ran up the steps and went in. She

heard voices in the parlour. Elizabeth had company. Jeanne must surely be abed by now. Lucy opened the parlour door and walked in. Elizabeth rose to greet her with a smile, and waved to the figure seated in shadow by the fire.

"We have a visitor from home, Lucy," she said, and the broad figure of Piers uncurled himself from the chair and stood up. In the firelight he looked even broader and taller, and more dark and serious than Lucy remembered him. Her heart gave a lurch of guilt as she remembered his letter, now hidden in one of her riding boots up in her chamber.

"How are you Lucy?" he said, and the warmth in his voice sent a tremor through her. It was in direct contrast to the unemotional tones of the Count, even when he was declaring love to her. Elizabeth lit the candles and Lucy could see how tired and drawn Piers looked, and that he was still wearing his travel-stained riding clothes.

"I am well, Piers, and you too, I hope?"

"Well, but tired," he answered. "It is late. If you will excuse me, I shall sleep now and we shall talk in the morning." He smiled and Elizabeth rose to lead him to a bedchamber.

"How is Thomas? And Rebecca? Is there plague still in London?" Lucy asked him as he was leaving.

"They are well, but the plague is still spreading, I fear. Many families have already left London, but Thomas is loth to forgo his visits to the Exchange to do business unless the situation becomes much worse. Rebecca plans to go to Longacre soon," Piers answered, then bade her good-night and followed Elizabeth out of the room.

Lucy sat by the fire and gazed into the flames. So the plague still spread. Were Molly and Garth still safe? In the dirty areas like Butcher's Row, one case in the lane could lead to the whole row being wiped out. Please God they would be spared. In the flames of the fire Lucy could picture Molly's scarred gentle face and the concern in her eyes, the concern she had tried to cover by pretending to be glad to get rid of Lucy, that last time they met. Tears blurred Lucy's sight as she thought of Molly and all her self-sacrifice.

The fire was dying down now, but one flame licked persistently round one last coal and in it Lucy could see Molly battling through flames to rescue an unknown baby.

The tears ran unashamedly down Lucy's cheeks now. Oh Molly! What an ungrateful beast I am! I had forgotten you till now, so wrapped up I was in my new happiness. Forgive me, Molly, I shall find you and make you happy again.

Elizabeth came softly into the room.

"Lucy, my dear, you're weeping," she said with deep concern in her voice. "Has that German Count said aught to upset you?"

"No, no, Elizabeth," Lucy replied, turning and taking Elizabeth's hand. "Do not concern yourself. I was thinking of old friends and how ungrateful I am. But I mean to put matters right when we return to England."

And for the first time Lucy told Elizabeth the whole of her story, of Molly and how she rescued Lucy from the fire.

"It was a hot, sultry night in August, and Molly had always said that date – August the fourteenth – is my birthday. My birth sign thus is Leo, the lion, and I am ruled by the sun. Molly says she never knew my real birth date, but this sign suited my hot nature best, and anyway, as far as she was concerned, I was born of the flames."

Elizabeth smiled as she too gazed at the embers in the hearth.

"Yes, I think a fiery sign becomes you,

Lucy. I hope you find Molly safe and well on our return; we shall take good care of her then. Come, it is late, let us go to bed."

She paused at the door. "One thing, Lucy. Do not tell Piers that you pretended to be me. He might tell Thomas, and I would not have Thomas think me deceitful."

"Then I'll not tell him," Lucy smiled, "for if I know Piers he would only reproach me for posing as a lady in earnest. He did not mind when it was only to tease Toby, but this is a different kettle of fish. And I am not anxious to be scolded, for Piers has a whip-like tongue when he's a mind to it."

She laughed, but inwardly she was glad Elizabeth did not know of the Count's proposal of marriage, in the mistaken belief that Lucy was a lady. This was a problem she had to solve for herself in the course of the next few days.

Piers was to spend only two days with the girls, for he had to conduct Thomas's business and return to England very soon. Lucy was relieved that the Count had promised to leave her alone until the end of the week. At least he and Piers would not meet, and her masquerade be discovered.

The following day Lucy found herself at last alone with Piers in the warm sunshine that filtered into the parlour. Elizabeth had gone to the kitchen to see Jeanne about the evening meal.

"Lucy – the letter," Piers said quickly. "I haven't had a chance to speak with you alone until now – did you deliver the letter I entrusted to you at Dover?"

Lucy's embarrassed face looked floor-wards.

"I'm sorry, Piers," she said in a low voice, her cheeks flushed with shame. How could she explain her tardiness? To explain her attentions from the Count, would mean having to admit her masquerade as Elizabeth.

"You mean – you have it still?" exclaimed Piers, his dark eyebrows raised in question. Lucy felt ashamed; Piers had trusted her, and she had let him down.

"I regret, it was not possible to deliver it secretly," she said. "I can only hope that not too much damage has been done by the delay."

"Give it to me, Lucy," he said quietly. By his tone she could not tell if he felt reproach or disappointment. Miserably she went to her chamber and returned with the letter. Piers took it eagerly, scanned the seal, then put it away in his pocket.

Elizabeth returned before Lucy could summon up sufficient courage to ask Piers again just how important the letter was. He said no more about it, so she assumed he was to deliver it himself since she had proved so untrustworthy.

"I have to go out now, Elizabeth," he said, turning to her with a smile, "but I shall be back for supper. Then early to bed for tomorrow I rise early to begin the journey home. Perhaps you will play the virginals for us this evening? And show me what you have painted since you came to Paris."

Elizabeth flushed prettily. "Oh, they're not very good, Piers. Except for a water colour of Lucy I have nearly finished. That reminds me – I need some more paints to finish it. Lucy, would you be so kind as to go with Piers into the town and bring them for me?"

Lucy looked at Piers. His smile faded fractionally, then returned. "I should be glad to take you, but there I must leave you, I fear."

They drove into the city in silence. Piers descended, insisting that Lucy kept the coach, and strode away. Lucy made Elizabeth's purchases quickly, then walked along the street. The sun had dipped and gone, and dusk was falling early. Already the people in the shops and inns were beginning to light their candles.

Lucy retraced her steps until she could see the coach along the street. She beckoned to the coachman, who whipped up the horses and trotted down to meet her.

As she climbed into the carriage, Lucy's eyes came level with the latticed windows of 'Le Chat Fidèle', a busy little inn. With a flash of recognition she saw the curly dark hair and handsome face of – Sir Toby! Lucy leaned forward in her seat and watched him. Forgetting to give the coachman any order, she stared, wondering why on earth Toby was in Paris.

Across the table from him his companion's head came into view. Lucy sat back with a start – it was Piers, and he was holding a paper in his hand. Then she saw the red seal. It was the letter he had asked her to deliver.

She saw him clutch it, talking earnestly to Toby, who nodded. Then he broke the seal, read quickly through the letter, and passed it over to Toby. He read it in turn and passed it back to Piers. Both men looked grave.

Suddenly Piers threw back his head and laughed, and held the paper to the flickering candle on the table. Flames enveloped it, and Piers twisted and turned it until no shred of it was left.

Stunned, Lucy drew back into the shadow of the coach, and rapped to the coachman to proceed.

Had the letter been of such small importance after all? Had he just been making a fool of her? Lucy was still perplexed when Piers came home to supper. He was gayer than she had ever seen him before, and actually sang in a strong baritone voice when Elizabeth played the virginals.

Lucy's curiosity could not be contained. As they prepared to retire, and Elizabeth was the first to leave the room, Lucy clutched Piers' arm.

"For heaven's sake, tell me. The letter – was it important or not? Are you angry with me, Piers, that I failed you?"

She looked up at him and could not know how appealing she looked, her green eyes wide and the auburn gleam of her hair reflecting the candlelight. Piers regarded her seriously. Then he put his arm around her shoulder.

"A letter from His Majesty is no slight matter, Lucy, but have no fear, no harm has been done by your failing to deliver it. And I beg you to remember, speak of this to no-one."

He tightened his hold on her shoulders, and Lucy thrilled to his touch. "Do not worry, I am not angry with you – quite the contrary. I am indebted to you, Lucy." And he bent and kissed her swiftly on the cheek, and was gone.

Lucy put her fingers to her cheek, which burned where Piers had kissed it. She trembled from head to foot, and as she doused the candles and went to the stairs, her head swam. Piers had kissed her! Out of gratitude, it was true, but what a storm it caused in her! Lucy knew then that this man who had scorned and mocked her, then trusted her and she had failed him, had awoken something in her that no man had ever done before.

But had she failed him? She had seen him with her own eyes destroying the letter, so it would seem he did not want it to be delivered. And he had said it was from the King. The Armytage family and Sir Toby's were all staunch Royalists and had remained so throughout the Lord Protector's reign when Charles Stuart was exiled abroad, so why should Piers and Toby destroy a letter from the King?

Unless they were traitors. Sick fear

clutched at Lucy's heart. Now she knew she felt something strong, something remarkably like affection for Piers, she had to discover at the same time that he was disloyal.

CHAPTER 9

The next morning Piers departed for England. For the remainder of the week Lucy could not bring herself to think of her problem with Count Reichendorf and his proposal. Her brain could only register one thought – she was in danger of falling in love with a man who was apparently worthless. Elizabeth remarked on her unwonted quietness, and Lucy longed to pour out her troubles. But knowing how it would upset Elizabeth, she kept silent.

Gradually her sick disappointment gave way to resentment and anger. Why should Piers make her fall in love with him? She *would* not love him, she would fight it. There were others as good as he, if not better. Paris was full of men who found her attractive – the Count, for instance. He was charming and attentive, and moreover, he had declared her fascination for him. Damn it! She would encourage the Count, and hang Piers!

Friday came, and with it, the Count. He rode alongside Lucy in the Bois de Vincennes, the steam from his horse's nostrils mixing with that of Lucy's horse. The air was soft and warm and the trees in leaf. Spring was clearly here at last and Lucy felt her spirits rising along with the sap.

At length the Count could wait no more. "I pray you, tell me Elizabeth, did you consider what I said to you?"

"I did, Count Reichendorf," Lucy replied.

"And your decision?" He turned and looked hard at her. Lucy allowed her horse to canter on a few more paces.

He spurred his horse on to draw level with her. "Well?"

"You are aware this is a decision not to be made lightly?" Lucy said.

"Of course."

"And also that even though a marriage may not yet be a physical union, nevertheless vows have been made and exchanged?" she went on.

"But in the circumstances they are not binding," the Count argued.

"No? Do you yourself lightly break your word after making such a promise, Count

Reichendorf?"

The Count reined in his horse. Lucy did likewise.

"I am a man of honour, Fräulein," he said icily. "I never give a promise unless I intend to keep it."

He slid down from his horse and came to help Lucy dismount. Then he led her into a little arbour, several of which were scattered around the Bois, to afford shelter from the weather. Out of the breeze, Lucy slipped off her hood and shook her hair free. The Count tethered the horses and came to stand beside her.

He really was remarkably handsome, Lucy thought to herself, with the sunlight gleaming on his blond hair. A trifle too detached and cold, perhaps, for her liking, but nevertheless a fitting substitute for Piers, now he had failed her so. There – Piers was in her thoughts again! Angrily she dismissed him from her mind.

"You understand then, Count Reichendorf, as a man of honour, promises must be kept. I am glad you are in agreement with me. I should be glad of your charming company as long as I remain in Paris, but as a friend only."

The Count turned sharply away. Over his

shoulder he said gruffly, "I understand and respect your feelings, my lady, I shall be honoured to continue to escort you. But I shall not give up hope that you may yet change your mind."

"Come and sit beside me," Lucy said gently. He was so charming, she could not be harsh with him. "Let us talk of other things."

After a moment's silence, the Count spoke. "Have you heard the news from England?" he asked.

"What news?" said Lucy with a start.

"Your King has declared war on the Dutch. The Dutch admiral, Opdam, had the effrontery to send his ships into the Thames and set fire to some of your ships."

Lucy's eyes opened wide in alarm. The Count's face softened as he smiled.

"Have no fear, your noble Duke of York engaged the Dutch fleet and vanquished them utterly. Twenty ships I am told he has sunk, including the Dutch admiral's flagship. London must be delirious with joy at the news, I should imagine."

"As indeed I am too!" Lucy declared. For however she might despise Piers, she was glad for his sake that the Channel now held no danger for him on his return to England.

Soon spring in Paris was turning into a hot and airless summer. Count Reichendorf seemed to have accepted Lucy's decision, and continued to escort her, to see the Sorbonne, the royal gardens, the Tuileries and the Jesuits' College, and to picnics on the lush sunsoaked banks of the Seine. By evening he was her gallant companion at every party and ball that Paris society had to offer. For Lucy it would have been a blissful summer, but for one matter.

Thomas wrote to Elizabeth regularly. Lucy, waiting avidly for news of Piers, heard only that he and Rebecca spent much time together, painting or riding or visiting friends.

"I hope he has a softening effect on Rebecca," Elizabeth would say to Lucy. "She had such a sharp tongue, and to be quite honest, I'm not looking forward to going home and being mistress of Kempston House. I would love it if I were in sole charge, but Rebecca has become accustomed to being mistress for so long. I do so hope being with Piers will make her more willing to accept me."

Lucy's feelings towards Rebecca were decidedly acid. She disliked the idea of her being unkind to Elizabeth, and she realised too that she resented her having Piers all to herself. But why should she? She had already made up her mind that Piers was a traitor and thus no longer interested her. But the memory of his kiss on her cheek made her raise her fingers to the spot once more, and again she could feel the skin tingle.

As the hot days wore on, Thomas's letters to Elizabeth became fewer and shorter. He asked Elizabeth to tell Lucy he had been unable to trace Molly to give her any money, as many people had now left London on account of the plague. Butcher's Row was almost deserted, because the occupants had either died or fled.

Elizabeth went visibly paler as she read out the letter. "I had not heard the plague had come again so badly," she said. "Oh I pray Thomas has the sense to leave his business now and move back to Longacre! I must write to him at once!"

By mid-September Thomas wrote, "I fear you are right, Elizabeth, and I must go to Longacre. Rebecca has been there some weeks already, and Piers comes and goes between us. No shops are open now, and no business is to be done on the Exchange. The King has removed the Court to Oxford.

"This week ten thousand poor souls have perished in London and the sights are too terrible to behold. Barely a house remains without the dreaded red cross on it; coffins lie exposed in the streets, for the vergers gave over the futile attempt to bury all the dead long ago. In this heat, the stench is unbearable.

"Last month when four thousand a week were dying, His Majesty called for a solemn fast throughout the country to soften God's displeasure, but such is the enormity of our sinfulness that the number increases daily.

"Hardly a soul walks the grass-grown streets now. Those that do are already crazed with terror and horror, and know no longer what they are doing. The only sounds to be heard in this silent city are the moans of the dying and the rumbling carts at night, which come to carry away the dead to the massive pits dug for them outside the city walls.

"Jennet is half mad now, I fear. Her family all died in a week, and I thank God she was here and so escaped the contagion. Mrs. Platt, Carew and Old Mother Benson are well but I hear your dressmaker, Mistress Buckley, perished with the rest of her family."

Thomas went on to say that, with a mind to the situation in London, it would be wiser if Elizabeth delayed her return to England if matters continued so gravely.

"Oh Lucy!" cried Elizabeth. "I would I were home now with Thomas! He needs me – I wish he had not bidden me stay here. He's so unmindful of himself, I should be there to care for him!"

Lucy was no less anxious. If Molly were not to be found, did that mean she had gone – or died? Oh no! Dear God, don't let Molly die so miserably, alone! she prayed, please save her! And take care of Piers too, whatever he may be, keep him and Thomas safe from harm!

Sadly Lucy realised she did care what befell Piers. He could be a traitor, a rogue, a thief, a murderer even, but she wanted him alive and well. And she'd scratch cousin Rebecca's eyes out before letting her have him!

Despite her anxiety Lucy laughed to herself. Imagine thinking of attacking a rival! She might be a fine lady to all appearances now, but the habits of a tavern maid died hard. Underneath the fine plumage, Lucy was still the fiery wench from the Tabard whom Garth had tried so gently but unsuccessfully to tame.

Count Reichendorf was unaccountably quiet on their next ride through the Bois. This time the leaves were falling, and the horses' hooves crackling over them was the only sound for some time.

"Come now, Count, why so thoughtful today?" Lucy teased him. "I usually expect more enlivening company from you. Is there something amiss?"

The Count eyed her in silence a moment.

"Your stay in France is nearly at an end, Elizabeth," he said. "When do you expect to return to England?"

"I do not yet know," Lucy replied airily, "but I expect it will be soon."

The Count leaned over and caught her bridle, then turned both horses' heads towards the arbour where they had talked once before.

As Lucy leaned into his arms to dismount, she saw a look of quiet determination in his eyes. He lowered her slowly, then ignoring the horses who stood still, cropping the grass, he kept his hold on her. Lucy looked up at him.

"Thank you, Count," she said by way of dismissal. Keeping hold of one arm, he drew her into the arbour. Then without warning, he gathered her close to him and kissed her, full and hard on her lips.

Lucy reacted violently. Her first feeling was one of disgust, from his hot, uncouth touch, and her second was of anger. She struggled, but he was far stronger than she, and would not let her go. Furious, she bit his lip, as hard as she could. Instantly, his hold relaxed and he stepped back, clutching his mouth.

"How dare you!" Lucy shouted. "You oaf, you braggart! And to think I took you for a gentleman!"

The Count stood, dabbing at the blood on his lips, his eyes wide in astonishment.

"Why did you do that?" Lucy demanded angrily. "Did I ever give you reason to suppose I would welcome such advances?"

"You did not give anyone to suppose you would *not* welcome them, Fräulein," he replied quietly. "Your behaviour in all the time I have known you has been coquettish, and your English Court life is renowned for its licentiousness. When I once spoke of this life to you, you assured me you found it amusing."

"To behold, Count Reichendorf, not to indulge in!" Lucy stormed at him, and bent to retrieve her riding crop which had fallen to the ground. Then she paced angrily up and down the arbour, trying to compose her thoughts.

"Lady Elizabeth, you are the most beautiful woman I have ever seen," the Count said seriously. For the first time there was real emotion in his voice, Lucy noticed with surprise. "If you could only see yourself now as I see you, your beautiful green eyes flashing fire and your hair tossing red and angry in the sunlight, then you could perhaps forgive my ardour. Never before in my life, I swear, has a woman created such fire in me as you do. In my madness for you I acted as I did. But I cannot promise to control myself much longer."

"But you must promise," Lucy declared, "or I shall not see you again."

"I repeat, I cannot promise, Elizabeth. If this strange obsession I have to possess you is love, then I love you. I must have you," he murmured, and moved closer. "Will you consider marrying me?" he said, "for have you I must, one way or the other, my little English fire-maiden."

"I cannot!" Lucy backed away from him, and raised her crop in warning as he came nearer. "Do not touch me!" she cried.

He laughed softly. She saw a light in his

eye she had seen before in the Tabard days. Suddenly he lunged forward and caught her, the crop pressed between their bodies. His lips sought her neck, her ears and her face, but Lucy twisted and struggled. She felt the cloth of her gown giving way at the seam as his feverish hands tore at her. Stubbornly she pulled at the trapped crop as she continued to struggle, and as she finally managed to wrest it free, the Count threw her off balance and fell on her on the ground. He laughed aloud.

"You're a tantalising, wanton, flame-spewing woman, Elizabeth, and far too good for any English merchant. Methinks I shall have a prior claim on you now, for your bond with your husband is still unconsummated!"

There was no doubting the intention in his eyes, and his cruelly persistent hands. Purposefully Lucy drove the end of the riding crop up into his face. The Count howled with pain and knelt back, clutching his cheek. From alongside his nose, blood started to ooze slowly from the gash, and before he could open his mouth to speak, Lucy leapt to her feet and ran out the arbour.

Thank God he had not tethered the

horses! Without help it was difficult to mount, hampered as she was by voluminous skirts, but mercifully she was up before the Count emerged from the arbour.

Whipping up the horse, Lucy galloped away.

"Merciful heavens!" exclaimed Elizabeth when she saw Lucy. "Whatever has happened? Your cloak and gown are all torn and covered with mud! Are you injured, Lucy?"

"No, no, Elizabeth, do not fret. I had a fall from my horse but fortunately it was on the fallen leaves in the Bois, so I was unharmed."

"Thank heaven for that!" said Elizabeth gratefully, then added, "I have news for you, Lucy."

"News?" said Lucy, her heart lurching. London – the plague – was Thomas or Piers stricken, she wondered tearfully.

"A letter from Thomas," Elizabeth replied happily. "He is sending Piers this week to come and fetch us home."

CHAPTER 10

Fortunately the Count did not reappear that week as Lucy and Elizabeth hastily packed and prepared to depart. No doubt he was nursing his wounded face, Lucy thought, hiding a scar which had not been honourably gained in battle or duel.

"Why such haste?" Elizabeth asked of Piers when he arrived. "I understood Thomas wanted us to bide here till the plague was safely over."

"It is only the last few cases that remain, the worst is past. Even the King is preparing to move his Court back to London," Piers answered. "But the relationship between England and France is becoming somewhat strained of late. King Charles's negotiations with King Louis are not going well, and there are fears France may well honour her treaty with Holland and prepare for war with our country. So it were best you left here quickly."

Lucy had never seen Elizabeth so animated.

"I am so happy to be going home to Thomas, Lucy. Oh, I shall be such a good wife to him! I have had some time abroad as my mother wished, and I feel it has been worth while; Jeanne has taught me much. Now I am ready to be mistress of Kempston House."

Lucy was glad to be returning to London too. Although she had enjoyed the gay social whirl of Paris matters had become somewhat out of hand with Count Reichendorf, and she was relieved to be able to escape without seeing him again. How she had been misled by his courtesy and charm! He had seemed so different from other men she had met, so much more concerned with intellectual matters than with physical pleasures. Yet he had attempted to ravish her, and believing her to be a married lady of rank too.

Lucy sighed. All men, it would seem, were brutes or, at the least, vain, self-seeking creatures. In both the Count and in Piers she had believed and then been betrayed.

She looked at Piers, deep in conversation with Elizabeth. They were both standing framed in the window, Piers towering above

Elizabeth's pale golden head. Lucy noticed how his hair curled in tendrils on his broad, weather-tanned brow, and a gentle smile curved the corners of his lips as he talked.

"You have no right to appear so kind and noble," Lucy muttered to herself savagely, "you, who are so smooth, so self-confident and yet so treacherous." In her mind's eye she could see him again, burning the royal letter. Piers looked away from Elizabeth's upturned face at that moment, as if he had caught the drift of Lucy's thoughts.

"You have been very quiet, Lucy. Are you in thoughtful mood?" he asked.

Lucy made no answer. Elizabeth spoke.

"Lucy had a fall from her horse a few days ago, and I think it has shaken her a little. She has been rather quieter than usual since then." She came to Lucy. "You are feeling up to the journey home, are you not, Lucy? I should be happy if we could depart at once, though I would not for the world incommode you. We shall delay a day or so if you would prefer it." She looked anxiously at Lucy.

"No, no," Lucy laughed reassuringly. "I am quite well. It was nothing. Come, let us finish our packing."

She was aware of Piers looking at her

curiously, but turned away to avoid meeting his intent dark gaze.

"Yes," he said briskly, "there is no time to be wasted."

Soon, having made their farewells and thanks to the Garennes, they were aboard the Calais-bound coach, ready for it to depart. Elizabeth and Lucy sat side by side amongst the other passengers while Piers saw to the loading of their luggage. In the torchlit yard of the 'Belle Sauvage' inn, ostlers and porters hurried to and fro. Lucy watched Piers, standing tall and erect amongst the scurrying figures.

Suddenly another man, cloaked and booted, strode out of the inn, his spurs clattering on the cobbled yard. In the gloom of the yard his tall figure was silhouetted against the light from the open doorway.

"Ho there!" he called in French. "Is there no-one to serve me a meal in this inn?" Lucy started. It was the Count's voice. She shrank back into the shadow of the coach, glad of the hood that shrouded her face.

Piers turned his head to inspect the owner of the voice, as the landlord darted back into the inn. "I come," the landlord said with an ingratiating smile. "What shall it be, sir? Roast beef, venison?"

The Count eyed Piers incuriously for a moment, and turned to follow the landlord indoors again. Lucy breathed a sigh of relief. Thank Heaven Elizabeth had never met the Count, although she knew about him. Awkward questions as to why Lucy did not speak to him, if only to say farewell, would inevitably have followed.

Lucy wished they would hurry and get the coach under way. Finally the door opened and Piers climbed in, and they were off, clattering across the cobblestones of a still and moonlit Paris.

Several days later Lucy and Elizabeth stood once again in the study of Kempston House. Piers was busy below helping Carew unload the carriage, and Thomas and Rebecca had not yet returned from Long-acre.

"Faugh! What a stench in here!" Lucy exclaimed, and crossed the room to the window. She threw back the latticed casements and turned to survey the room. What a different sight it presented from the first time she came here. Then it had been warm and alive, glowing with brass and polished furniture and a roaring log fire; now it had the cold, dank evil odour of a tomb.

"It is indeed a foul smell," Elizabeth

agreed, letting her hood slip back from her golden head. "But the house has been shut up and deserted. I am sure Thomas would have had it all cleaned and aired in readiness for our return, had we not been obliged to quit France so suddenly."

"No matter," Lucy said practically. "Mrs. Platt and Jennet and Carew are here now. They and I can soon have everything cleaned and scrubbed. These will have to be taken down and cleaned first," she said indicating the tapestries of the walls.

"And I shall help you," Elizabeth cut in. "I have learnt much about housekeeping, and as mistress I insist on having a hand in it," she said, seeing Lucy was about to protest. "It will give me much pleasure to see Thomas's face when he finds it is not damp and cheerless, but clean and warm and wholesome when he returns."

Thomas was indeed delighted when he arrived next day, saying Rebecca was to follow later. Lucy was touched to see his eyes light up with pleasure as Elizabeth threw herself into his arms to welcome him home.

"Oh Thomas, I have missed you so much," she said, her eyes shining, "but now I have so much more to bring you. I have the most wonderful receipts for preserves that Jeanne taught me, and for pickling, and so much else besides!"

"We shall have the most unusual table in London, I can see, with all your French cuisine, my dear," Thomas said with a gentle, doting smile as he led Elizabeth away to rest. Lucy sighed contentedly. It was wonderful to see them so content together. Thomas deserved a happy marriage after his generosity and forbearance, and Elizabeth would be a perfect match for him. This, she smiled to herself, was one man who did not come within her definition of men a week ago – all vain, self-seeking creatures – and she was glad for Elizabeth's sake.

She sat on the window seat where Elizabeth had talked so animatedly about her plans for the trip abroad so long ago. Through the latticed pane she could see London, lying quiet after the recent plague, like a sick man who has not yet recovered sufficient strength to stand up.

Piers entered the room and saw her. He stood and watched her for a moment.

"Dreaming?" he asked absently as he flung himself into a chair.

"Remembering," she replied coolly, looking directly at him.

"Your old way of life before you left London, you mean? Rather different for you now, is it not? No longer an aching belly and a blanket of frost o' nights, as you once told me."

"I am grateful to Thomas and Elizabeth for that," Lucy said, and looked away again.

"I seem to detect an icy tone in your voice, Lucy," Piers commented, looking across at her with his dark, penetrating gaze and his eyebrows arched. "May I presume to ask what it is that has caused you to behave so coldly towards me?"

Before Lucy could reply, the doors opened noisily and Rebecca swept in.

"I' faith, you might at least be gentleman enough to welcome me into the house, Piers," she exclaimed irritably, "instead of leaving me to cope alone downstairs!" She caught sight of Lucy in the window. "Ah Lucy! Go down and send Jennet up to me at once. And bid the child make haste if she doesn't want her ears to ring."

She turned her back on Lucy as a sign of dismissal. As Lucy made to go, she saw Piers rise to take Rebecca's cloak and kiss her warmly on the cheek. Lucy pulled the doors after her to close them.

"Good God!" Rebecca exclaimed breaking from Piers' embrace. "The tapestries, the coverings – they must be all soaked with the contagion! Why on earth has not the silly wench Elizabeth thrown them all out?"

Lucy felt a flush of anger flooding her face. She threw the doors open again.

"Elizabeth is not such a silly wench as you would wish to believe! She herself took a share in cleaning and scrubbing everything that is in this room," she cried out in protective anger. "So you need have no fear for your precious skin!"

She slammed the doors after her, breathing deeply in her fury. How dare that woman slander Elizabeth! She herself had watched Elizabeth, flushed and tired from exhaustion after her labours. Then that creature who had not lifted a finger to help her had the effrontery to call Elizabeth a silly wench! Lucy gathered up her skirts and hurried angrily towards the kitchen.

"Lucy!" a peremptory voice called. Lucy turned, to see Piers' angered look.

"You forget yourself, mistress," he said icily. It was like the crack of a whip.

"I do not care!" Lucy blazed. "I will not have her mock Elizabeth!"

"Your protective feelings do you credit," Piers said coldly, "but your travels abroad do not seem to have improved your manners, my lady. Remember always that you – are – a – servant – in – this – house. To speak disrespectfully to a member of the household will invoke your instant dismissal. You will apologise to Miss Rebecca immediately."

"I will not," Lucy flared. "It is she who should apologise to Elizabeth for wronging her!"

"And you are the creature who would ape the lady!" Piers mocked. "Your behaviour is as base as your origins, Lucy. You were and are still – a guttersnipe!"

It was a whiplash blow. Lucy reacted like a cornered cat. "You may call me what you will," she hissed at him, "but if you will not defend Elizabeth then I will!"

Piers gripped her by both wrists. "You are a wildfire wench, are you not? I respect your loyalty to Elizabeth but I will not have you offend my cousin Rebecca. She is furious with you, and rightfully so. You would be ill advised to incur her wrath any further, or you will perforce find yourself roaming the streets in search of another bed tonight. Apologise to her instantly."

Lucy wrenched her arms free. "No!" she cried.

"You choose the streets then?" Piers asked menacingly.

"I'd as willingly choose the streets as pander to that woman!" Lucy declared.

"I thought so," Piers said quietly. "So much for your much-vaunted virginity. I suspected as much when I saw you embracing Toby at Whitehall."

Lucy stared in disbelief. Oh no! He could not still believe her to be a whore! Before she realised what she was doing, Lucy's indomitable temper dictated her actions. She slapped Piers hard across his face.

She gasped when she realised what she had done. Piers' hand went slowly up to his reddening cheeks. For a moment, neither spoke.

"Madam, I thank you for opening my eyes to the truth," he said levelly. "I had almost been cozened into believing in your honesty. I had even begun to believe you were a warm-hearted, generous girl who might some day return my awakening affection. Now I know otherwise."

Lucy stood bewildered. What was he saying? Could she believe her ears? Was he saying he had been attracted to her, a maid from the gutters, as he constantly reminded her? Suddenly Piers spoke again, but this

140

time no longer coldly. There was suppressed fury in his voice.

"You would be well advised to have a care to your temper, Miss Lucy, or one day it may prove your undoing. You need a strong man to take you, wildcat, and may God help the man who takes on the task!"

And before Lucy could retort, Piers stopped her mouth by pressing down hard on it with his own. It was a hard, savage, bitter kiss, bruising her mouth and awakening her fury again. He was treating her like a wanton! She pummelled his chest, and kicked at his shins, but to no avail.

Lucy trembled and stopped struggling. Then she became conscious of the glorious, mounting, wildfire excitement burning inside her.

Suddenly Piers let her go free. "Blast you!" he muttered, and strode angrily away.

Sobbing with rage, Lucy ran out of the house.

CHAPTER 11

In the garden, Lucy flung herself full-length, still sobbing, on to the grass under a mulberry tree, and gave herself up to abandoned, hysterical weeping. She tore at the grass with her fingernails as she lay prostrate, and kicked furiously at the unresisting turf.

Much later, emotion spent, she sat up and mopped her face with the hem of her skirt. She realised she was cold and damp, unprotected from the bitterly chill night air in only a thin gown. She shivered, chafing her bare arms to restore some warmth to them.

She could not stay out like this all night, though in her anger and hatred of Piers she had vowed never to enter Kempston House again. But that was an hour ago. Her pride was a lesser force than her coldness at this moment.

But suppose they refused to allow her in again? Thomas and Piers would probably have agreed by now that such behaviour from a servant was intolerable, and Rebecca would no doubt be thirsting for her blood, or taking out her wrath on poor Jennet.

And what of Elizabeth? Lucy thought it was probable she had not yet been told of what had befallen, or she would surely have come in search of her friend. Just at this moment Lucy had sore need of a friend by her side. She had just come to realise how badly she had behaved. Piers had reminded her she was a servant, and it was true, that was her capacity in the Armytage household. The trouble was that being allowed to act as a lady, ordering what she wished and having her every whim indulged had spoilt her for the role of servant again.

It would have to be Rebecca who had goaded her beyond endurance. Rebecca liked Lucy no more than Lucy liked her, so it was certain she would ensure Lucy's dismissal. Apologising to Piers and Thomas would be useless; they would expect her to apologise to Rebecca too, and that was unthinkable.

Lucy paced fretfully to and fro on the terrace, undecided whether to go in or run

away. She could always go back to Southwark – and Molly, if she was to be found.
But she could not leave without explaining
her absence to Elizabeth.

Lucy's chattering teeth and increasing
numbness from the cold decided matters
for her. She would try to sneak in quietly
and hide in her own room, then face the
family in the morning.

But face Piers? Lucy hesitated with her
hand on the knob of the garden door. Piers
had shown her tonight how much he
despised her. Lucy ran the back of her hand
across her mouth again as though to wipe
away the memory of that burning, savage
kiss. She felt near to tears again, but this
time of self-pity, not anger, when she
recalled the glorious sensation his touch had
aroused in her. It was cruel that only then
had she discovered what feelings he stirred
in her, at the very moment he made it clear
he no longer cared about her and in fact
openly despised her.

Lucy sneezed violently. It was no use, she
would have to demean her pride and crawl
in, if only for much-needed warmth.

She reached the safety of her room without meeting anyone. She undressed quickly
and leapt into bed. Lord! It was marvellous

to be between warm blankets! But Lucy's limbs would not thaw out. She huddled up tightly, rubbing and blowing on her hands and arms, but all she could do was cough and shiver all night. Finally she fell into a fitful sleep.

Lucy woke early to find all the bedclothes tossed aside. She was burning from head to foot, but still shivering, and her head was throbbing with pain. Jennet slunk in, wild-eyed and fearful.

"Lady Elizabeth sent me to bid you go to her at once, Lucy," she whined. "Miss Rebecca's in a fearful state this morning, and demanding to see you."

"I know well the reason," Lucy muttered. Her tongue felt parched and swollen, and her voice issued as a croak. She sat on the edge of the truckle bed, holding her pounding head in her hands.

"Go tell Lady Elizabeth I come at once," she said, making to rise and dress, but her knees seemed to have no strength to bear weight. She tottered and fell at Jennet's feet.

"Oh Lawks! Lucy, get up!" Jennet whined piteously, "or you'll have Miss Rebecca angrier than ever, and I won't half pay for it then! Come on, Lucy," she coaxed, and when Lucy only lay and groaned, Jennet fell on her knees beside her and howled.

"What on earth is it?" Lucy heard Elizabeth's voice say in alarm, "Lucy! Jennet, don't just sit there, help Lucy back into bed! Oh my poor lamb! Whatever is it, Lucy love?"

Lucy was barely aware of Elizabeth lifting her into bed with Jennet's help, and covering her. "You have a high fever, Lucy. You must stay in bed. No, do not concern yourself about anything," Elizabeth said firmly as Lucy feebly attempted to sit up.

Gratefully, Lucy let everything slide away from her. Later, through a haze she became aware of Elizabeth bending over her, tenderly sponging her fevered forehead with cool water, of the sheets burning her aching body, and of disembodied faces peering at her and disappearing again.

Days and nights became indistinguishable to Lucy. Time did not exist in a hazy limbo of pain and parched heat. Only thoughts stayed alive, running on in a meaningless jumble. Again and again she heard the cracked voice of an aged crone shrieking scorn at Rebecca, who had locked a helpless child in a black tomb, wailing piteously for a pox-ridden Molly, and vowing hatred of all men.

Piers' face appeared to Lucy out of the mist. Instantly the old crone spat out her hate, and he faded away. Then a melodious voice soothed, "Come now, Lucy, drink this and rest," and a blissful coolness ran over Lucy's parched throat.

One day the fog cleared in Lucy's brain. Elizabeth was sitting by, sewing.

"The old woman, where is she?" Lucy whispered. Elizabeth rose at once and came to her.

"What old woman, love? There's no-one by but me."

"But I heard her, shouting and cursing," Lucy protested feebly.

"You have been delirious, Lucy. You must have imagined her," Elizabeth said gently, smoothing her pillows.

Then Lucy realised. It was her own voice she had heard. Dear heaven! What had she been saying? She could remember nothing save that it was vile talk, full of imprecations and curses. How she must have offended Elizabeth's gentle ears!

"I do not deserve a friend such as you, Elizabeth," she whispered gratefully, clutching her hand.

"Nonsense. They told me about that night you were taken ill. I shall never forget such loyalty," Elizabeth answered simply.

Slow tears of gratitude welled into Lucy's eyes. She felt unworthy of Elizabeth's friendship. To credit Lucy with loyalty was too much. Molly had figured largely in Lucy's nightmares of the last week, and how loyal had she been to Molly? Of all creatures in the world, Molly had sacrificed more for Lucy's sake than anyone else, and how much thought had Lucy given her while she had been enjoying life to the full?

For all Lucy knew, Molly could be starving, homeless or even dead of the plague, and Lucy had done nothing to help her. The least she could have done was to go to Southwark in search of Molly as soon as she had returned to London.

Lucy vowed to go the moment her legs were strong enough to carry her. With Elizabeth's tender ministrations the fever abated quickly and Lucy grew strong again. Christmas came and went. One day in the new year, Jennet sat with Lucy as they both busied themselves with the household mending.

"Tell me, Jennet," Lucy said curiously, "are you happy?"

Jennet looked up from her sewing, her mouth dropping open and her eyes staring.

148

Lucy felt a pang of pity for this unprepossessing child with her low brow, vacant face, and permanent need to breathe with her mouth open.

"What do you mean?" Jennet said.

"Do you like working here at Kempston House?"

Jennet considered for a moment, then shrugged her shoulders. "I suppose so. It's the only place I've ever worked. My mam and my brothers all died of the plague, so I've nowhere else to go anyway. Why do you ask?"

"How do you feel about the way Miss Rebecca treats you?"

Jennet's eyes widened. She glanced nervously over her shoulder and dropped her needle. She fumbled to retrieve it, and fell off her stool with a faint cry when Rebecca's voice was heard.

"Jennet! Jennet, where the devil are you? You foul little slut, come here this instant!" Rebecca's voice was coming closer. Jennet flung her sewing to the floor and fled.

Lucy heard Rebecca in the corridor outside scolding Jennet.

"What, dancing attendance on Madam Lucy, are you? I'll teach you whose maid you are," she heard her say. There followed a resounding crack and Jennet's voice rose in a wail. Angrily Lucy swung her legs out of bed, then stopped when she heard another low, commanding voice.

"That's enough. Downstairs to the kitchen, Jennet. Mrs. Platt will need your services to prepare supper." It was Piers. Lucy heard Jennet scuttling away, then Piers spoke again.

"There is no need to be brutal with the child, Rebecca. Bear in mind that she is an orphan now, and none too well-endowed with intelligence. Have a little patience with her, I beg you."

"What? When I find her coming out of that trollop's room?" Rebecca's scornful voice retorted. "It is enough that she is still in the house, without surrendering my maid to her as well."

Lucy burned with indignation. She heard Piers speak in a low voice, but could not make out the words. Slowly their footsteps receded.

It was obvious Lucy was no longer welcome in Kempston House. They had probably only suffered her to stay because of her illness. And after what she had said to them all in her delirium, the sooner she left here, the happier they would all be. Except

Elizabeth, perhaps, but even for Elizabeth's sake she could not stay in a house where her presence was resented, possibly even hated.

As long as she remained in bed, Lucy felt like a prisoner, trapped in a house together with Piers who despised her. It was a pity now that she felt so much more kindly disposed towards him since he protected Jennet from Rebecca. Rebecca's dislike of Lucy meant nothing to her, but for Piers to know she was still there she felt sure must cause him some displeasure.

So Lucy longed to be free, to gallop again in the Bois on horseback, the wind streaming through her long, free-flowing hair, if she and this family could not live happily together. Once she left, however, there would be no more horse riding or fine clothes and good meals. It would mean going back to the poverty of the Butcher's Row days. And losing Elizabeth's friendship.

Lucy sighed. It had to be done. At last, she was on her feet again. That morning Elizabeth hurried in.

"Piers was right! You remember he came to Paris to bring us home because it was feared Louis might declare war against England? Well, we have just heard he has done so."

Lucy had almost forgotten France. Everything that had happened before her illness seemed a lifetime away, but in truth it was barely two months since she and Elizabeth had come home to England.

France and war. Lucy felt uneasy. That letter Piers had burnt – he said it was from the King, but not to whom it was addressed. It was well known that King Charles doted on his younger sister, Henrietta, who was married to Louis' brother, the Duke of Orleans. Could the letter have been meant for her? Or for Louis himself?

She realised Elizabeth was still talking.

"So Toby has had to return to England quickly too."

"Toby?" asked Lucy. She had seen him in Paris that night with Piers, but Elizabeth had not known he was there.

"Yes. He has been travelling around Europe, and was in Paris when we were, oddly enough. Is that not a coincidence? He returned a few days ago and brought a friend home to stay with him. They have just come to visit Piers and they are together in the study now. Thomas has gone to the Exchange on business."

Elizabeth hurried away to see her guests. Dispiritedly Lucy made her bed, then followed downstairs. In the vestibule she heard Piers talking in the study, the door of which was standing ajar.

Now would be her opportunity to tell Piers of her intention to leave. She approached the door, until she could see Piers standing before Thomas's desk, addressing Toby who stood by the roaring log fire. A third man was sitting in a high-backed settle, his back to the door, and all Lucy could see of him was a pair of long, graceful legs, crossed at the knee.

"I remember now!" Piers exclaimed. "It was in Paris – at the Belle Sauvage."

"You mean you've met Hans before?" Toby said, eyebrows raised in surprise.

"Yes, I'm sure of it now. It was the night we were leaving for home, taking the Calais coach. We did not exactly meet, but I saw you there trying to get served with a meal."

"That is correct," a low voice from the settle replied.

"By 'r lady, that is indeed a coincidence!" exclaimed Toby. "Of all people I should befriend abroad, it should be one you have met before, Piers."

"There is no coincidence," the low voice went on. "When I realised you were a friend of Lady Elizabeth, Sir Toby, I made a point

153

of pursuing our acquaintanceship, in order to trace her here in London."

Toby looked startled. Piers' face was stern. Lucy shuddered with apprehension. It could not be!

But when the tall figure uncurled himself from the settle and stood face to face with Piers, Lucy saw it was indeed the smiling, mask-like face of Count Reichendorf!

CHAPTER 12

Lucy paced her room, her hands clammy with sweat. The Count here in London, in Kempston House! It was evident from what she had heard that he had used Toby to get to her – but under the impression she was the Lady Elizabeth!

What should she do? Her first impulse was to run away back to Southwark as she had planned, but to do so would be to leave Elizabeth in trouble with the Count. She would have to stay and admit the truth, that she had masqueraded as Elizabeth in France.

She shuddered as she thought of the reactions that would bring. Toby would probably roar with laughter, Elizabeth would be hurt that her honour had been impugned, poor Thomas would be puzzled and perplexed by it all, and Piers would be furiously angry. He had not approved of her pretending to be a lady the time they had hoaxed Toby, but now she had done it again, and this time dishonoured Elizabeth, his anger would know no bounds. His protective love of Elizabeth had always been the quality in him that Lucy admired most.

Elizabeth opened the door. "Still here, Lucy? I thought you were coming downstairs. I am just about to serve some refreshment to the gentlemen in the study – come and join us there."

Lucy hesitated. She must do what she knew to be right, and clear Elizabeth's name with Piers and the Count, but not with Elizabeth there to be shamed.

"Please come, Lucy," Elizabeth coaxed, mistaking her hesitation. "Rebecca will be joining them too in a moment, and I would prefer not to be the only other woman there. She is such lively, scintillating company, she makes me a poor, featureless creature by comparison."

"That she could never do," Lucy turned and took her by the shoulders. "She'll never have half the love and sympathy and understanding you have. Oh Elizabeth!" Lucy felt deeply ashamed. Of all the people in the world she had to hurt, it had to be Elizabeth!

"What is it, Lucy?" Elizabeth was perplexed.

"I'm so ashamed. How can I tell you? And Piers – he despises me enough, already."

"Piers? He does not despise you, Lucy. On the contrary, he was deeply concerned for you while you were ill. He came and sat with you often, and bathed your forehead and looked to your wants, so that I could rest. Oh Lucy, if you had seen him then, foregoing his sleep to sit all night, you would not doubt his genuine concern for you."

Lucy looked at her in surprise. Piers had done that? Momentarily her heart warmed to him again, then the feeling waned as she imagined what he would say when she made her confession. But Elizabeth must be kept out of it.

"Elizabeth, I must speak to Piers and Toby, but I would prefer to do it alone. Would you grant me a favour, and let me have five minutes alone with them before you come?"

"But of course, if you wish," said Elizabeth, but Lucy could see she was puzzled why Lucy should not wish to share the secret with her.

"Thank you," Lucy said and kissed her cheek.

Standing outside the study door, Lucy could see the man by the fire.

"I regret my brother is out on business, but in any case I fear there must have been some mistake," Piers was saying. "It could not possibly have been the Lady Elizabeth you are speaking of."

"There is no mistake, Herr Armytage," the Count replied stiffly. "It was Elizabeth, Lady Sherdley, otherwise Mistress Armytage. We spent much time together in Paris, and she made such an impression on me I would have her for my wife."

On the Count's face, half-turned towards her, Lucy could see the white scar on his cheek gleaming in the firelight.

"Even if my lady behaved as you say – which I will not believe – she is already married," Piers pointed out.

"But was not then?" the Count replied.

"What do you mean?"

"She was still a virgin wife. The marriage was still unconsummated."

Piers hesitated. "That is irrelevant – now. She has been home three months," he said, turning away. He no doubt wished he could eject this troublesome intruder, Lucy thought, but was containing himself because it was Toby's friend.

"Ah yes," the Count said amiably, "but mine, I believe, was the prior right." He smoothed the lace ruffles on his sleeve with a satisfied smile.

Piers turned sharply. "What the devil do you mean by that, sir?" he said in a low menacing voice.

The Count smiled again. "Well, shall we say the lady Elizabeth granted her favours to me first? That, I think, gives me a prior claim."

Piers' face darkened and Lucy saw him bit his lip in anger. She was too stunned to move.

"Aha! So now we are eavesdropping on private conversations, are we?" a smoothly acid voice at her elbow said. Rebecca stood there, smiling malevolently. "Not content with the trouble you have caused already, eh? And all the fuss, nursing a sick tavern wench back to health. You have received far better treatment than you deserved, thanks to a soft-hearted master. Get downstairs to the kitchen where you belong, and cause us no more trouble."

She stood aside to let Lucy pass. Lucy turned back to the study door.

"Did you hear me?" Rebecca snapped.

"There is something I must do," said

159

Lucy, and pushed the door open.

Piers looked up sharply. "What is it?"

"I must speak with you a moment, sir," Lucy said.

Rebecca pushed past her. "Piers, for heavens' sake, make this creature do as I say. She has refused to go to the kitchen as I bade her. I found her listening at the door."

"Lucy, go below," Piers ordered quietly.

"But sir, it is imperative I speak with you," Lucy began. "It is vital, I cannot go and leave you under a false..."

"Be silent, Lucy!" Piers thundered. "How dare you defy me! Go downstairs!" Lucy hesitated, then turned to go. "Rebecca, be so kind as to leave us a moment, will you?" Lucy heard him say as she left. "There is a matter of supreme importance for us to discuss. I would be much obliged."

Rebecca withdrew, giving Lucy a smile of malicious triumph as she swept past her in the corridor.

Lucy was in a turmoil. She must let Piers know of Elizabeth's innocence somehow, but when? And how? One thing was certain – she could not run away until she had cleared the matter up.

Elizabeth was bubbling that evening. "Rebecca has taken a fancy to the handsome friend of Toby's – I forget his name, a Count with a strange German name rather like that one you once used to speak of in Paris. Anyway, she is hoping Piers will invite him to join them again in the study later. They've been busy talking business, something to do with Thomas's exports, probably. She has had Jennet curl her hair again and press her best gown, so eager she is to impress the Count."

"You think Rebecca is in search of a suitable husband then?" Lucy smiled.

"Gracious no!" Elizabeth exclaimed in surprise. "Rebecca likes all men to be impressed by her dark, dramatic beauty so that compliments flow, but she has only one man in mind to marry."

"She has?" It was Lucy's turn to be surprised. She had not thought Rebecca was determined to marry, and even less that she had one particular man in mind.

"Oh yes. She has made it clear that she plans one day to marry her cousin Piers."

Piers – and Rebecca? It did not at first speculation seem possible! Rebecca, the acid, cruel, selfish woman, and sensitive Piers!

"Does Piers return her feeling?" Lucy could not resist asking Elizabeth.

"I know not," Elizabeth replied, "he does not make me his confidante. As you know, Piers talks little of his feelings. All I know is that whatever he feels, he feels deeply. He is a man of great sensitivity, as his paintings show."

Lucy remembered the portraits he had painted of Thomas and Rebecca, and which hung in the gallery upstairs. There was infinite affection in his portrayal of Thomas's gentleness, and the one of Rebecca was an exact reproduction of her haughty beauty.

"Thomas tells me Piers and Rebecca have spent much time in Piers' studio this last year while she sat for him again," Elizabeth went on. "I dare say we shall see the finished product ere long."

Lucy turned away, stinging jealousy pricking at her. So it was true. Piers was too good for Rebecca, she cried out inwardly. But then, she was forgetting; he was apparently a traitor. No amount of virtuous qualities in him could atone for that if he was. But Lucy falteringly had to admit to herself that even this heinous crime could not blacken him in her eyes. She had seen his tender protectiveness towards Elizabeth, and again for Jennet, and now to her shame she knew he had ministered to her in her illness, despite her delirious savagery to him.

Later in the evening Lucy came upstairs from the kitchen. In the vestibule Piers was talking earnestly to Toby.

"This is my affair, Toby. I do not wish a breath of it to reach Thomas's ears, you understand?" Piers broke off suddenly when he saw Lucy. "You will bid Elizabeth goodnight before you go?" he went on to Toby. "She is in the parlour I think."

Toby went into the parlour. Piers looked quickly at Lucy, then made to go off down the corridor.

"Master Piers, I pray you let me speak with you now," Lucy said earnestly.

Piers turned slowly. "I would have thought after our last meeting alone, you would never have wished to speak to me again, Lucy."

Lucy caught her breath as she remembered that bitter kiss. She looked at the floor in embarrassment a moment, then recalled the urgency of her message. "I had forgot, almost. Forgive me. But there is something else..."

"Forgive you?" Piers said in surprise. "It is I who should beg your forgiveness, Lucy, for treating you so. You deserved reproach for your behaviour to Rebecca, as you would admit but for your fiery pride, but not such treatment. It was your hot temper that undid me."

"I beg you, forget the incident sir, as I have done..."

"You did not forget it lightly, Lucy. In your illness you said much of how you felt towards me after that night."

"Delirium, sir, but please listen to me!"

"What is it, Lucy?" he said kindly, as if anxious to please her now.

"The matter of lady Elizabeth and Count Reichendorf, I can explain it all," Lucy began.

Piers' eyes glazed over suddenly. He gripped Lucy's shoulders.

"Silence! You are not to breathe their names together again, do you hear? Nor mention this matter again – ever – to anyone!" His voice was low, but determination glittered menacingly in it.

"But sir, you have not heard the truth of it!"

"Lucy! I forbid you to speak!" he thundered.

"I must!"

"Lucy," he continued more quietly, laying his fingers on her lips, "the happiness of several people is involved, not least of them Elizabeth's. If you have any love for me, I beg you to hold your tongue now, and speak not another word on the subject." Lucy hung her head. "Do not worry, I have the matter in hand," he added.

What should she do? Obey Piers and leave Elizabeth under suspicion or defy him in order to clear her? Toby came out into the vestibule. Piers let go of Lucy and went to accompany him to the door. Lucy began to climb the stairs.

"Goodnight, Lucy," Toby called, "and goodnight to you too, Piers. Till dawn on Friday. I shall call for you."

"No need," Piers replied quietly. "Meet me at Hyde Park."

"Where we shall no doubt find the Count waiting," Toby laughed.

Lucy stopped on the stairs. Piers meeting the Count in the Park? Had they sorted the matter out then and settled their differences? To be meeting at dawn could only mean they were going riding together, and Lucy knew how much the Count enjoyed a morning canter. It was strange though, after the recent tension between them she had witnessed.

As she undressed she puzzled over it, but

could not fathom it out. She shrugged her shoulders. No matter. Whatever the explanation, it would seem matters had been settled amicably, and Elizabeth's honour was no longer in question.

If that were so, then Lucy was at least free to leave Kempston House. She would explain to Elizabeth tomorrow, and then make ready to go.

CHAPTER 13

Lucy rose early and went to Elizabeth's room, feeling very dejected. She knew Elizabeth would be very disappointed, and Lucy only hoped she would not see her leaving as a further betrayal.

Elizabeth, already up, sat brushing her hair listlessly. "Good morrow, Lucy," she said, smiling faintly. "Come, sit by me and brush my hair."

Lucy took the brush and lightly stroked the long golden tresses. "Elizabeth, I fear I must leave you and go back to Southwark whence I came," she said tentatively.

Elizabeth uttered a cry and turned on her stool to face Lucy. "Oh Lucy, are you unhappy here? Is it Rebecca?"

"No, not Rebecca," Lucy interrupted. "You remember I told you about Molly, and that I must go and search for her when I could? Now is the time, Elizabeth. I fear I have left it too long already."

"Thomas tried to trace her for you when we were in Paris," Elizabeth reminded her. "She no longer lived in Butcher's Row."

"I know, and am grateful, but there are other places I can try; friends who may know of her whereabouts," Lucy explained. "And there are other reasons..."

"Other reasons? What reasons, Lucy?" Elizabeth asked.

"It is difficult to explain, but I think – people would be happier if I were out of the way," Lucy said with downcast eyes.

"It *is* Rebecca who has hurt you!"

"No, truly Elizabeth. It is true she does not care for me, nor I for her, but that is not the reason. I have let you down – I cannot explain how – and Piers too. It would be better if I went away. And I *must* find Molly." Lucy got up and paced around the room, awaiting the reproaches or the pleading she felt sure must come from Elizabeth.

But Elizabeth did not speak and Lucy walked slowly back to her, looking directly at her for the first time. Elizabeth was paler, far paler than usual.

"Elizabeth? Have I upset you?" Lucy said, kneeling before her and taking her hands.

Elizabeth smiled, "No, not you. I am sad if you must leave, but when you have found

Molly, you will come back to me, will you not? It is but a temporary parting." Lucy did not answer at once.

"Then why are you so pale and quiet, Elizabeth? Is aught amiss?"

Elizabeth spread her hands. "I know not what it is. I think I am a little tired, that is all."

"Of course! You are exhausted after nursing me so long. How thoughtless of me to think of leaving you! It is you who need caring for now," Lucy cried.

"No, no, I am not ill. You must go seek Molly, Lucy, or your conscience will give you no peace. In the meantime I shall rest quietly until you return."

Lucy agreed to set off the following day. Nevertheless she felt uneasy about leaving Elizabeth, always so fragile and uncomplaining, in order to look for Molly. Heaven! How did one decide, when one's loyalties conflicted!

During the night she was awakened by Elizabeth. "I was so restless, I could not sleep," Elizabeth explained. Lucy helped her curl up in a fur rug and rest on the end of Lucy's bed. Elizabeth began to talk of the coming spring, and what they would do.

"And we shall finish the water colour of

you I began in Paris, and ride in the Ring in Hyde Park so that we may see the fashions at Court since we left," she said, some of her former gaiety returning.

"The Ring? What is that?" said Lucy stifling a yawn.

"It's a large circle in the centre of the park where the fashionable people ride in coaches or on horseback, and greet each other and talk. Rather like Pall Mall, remember, the day we went to St. James's Park?"

Lucy nodded; her head felt very heavy.

"When I first came to London Thomas took me riding there," Elizabeth continued, "and I saw the King with his brother, the Duke of York; such gaiety and happy talk there was, such fine silks and velvets, and gold lace and jewellery. It was the most wonderful sight I had ever beheld, and I was delighted by it. Until Thomas told me the Ring was frequently used for other, less pleasant reasons," Elizabeth added, "and then I did not find it quite so attractive."

"What other reasons?" asked Lucy sleepily.

"It was a fine, sunny afternoon when we rode there, but Thomas said that often in the dawn mists the Ring is the meeting place of those who have a difference to settle and can only discover one way to settle their quarrel." She looked across at Lucy. "It is terrible, is it not, when men can resolve their quarrels only with a sword, and have to resort to duelling? But I gather that frequently happens in London, and usually in Hyde Park."

She chattered on then in lighter vein on other topics, but Lucy did not hear her. She was thunderstruck by the sudden realisation of the significance of Piers' and the Count's meeting in the Park. Elizabeth did not know that she had just revealed to Lucy what was to happen at dawn on Friday – tomorrow!

And Lucy had been foolish enough to believe that Piers and the Count had somehow resolved the problem of Lady Elizabeth without it coming to light. What a fool she had been to think they had become friends!

Not only did the problem still exist, but Piers' life was in danger if he took part in the duel! Lucy would have to put a stop to it, come what may.

Lucy forced her eyes open. A greying light was framed in the window. She tried to beat back the mist in her brain. Elizabeth lay down beside her and began breathing deeply and regularly.

"What time is it?" Lucy asked.

"Near dawn, I think," murmured Elizabeth sleepily.

Lucy leapt to her feet, swayed, and caught the bedpost to steady herself. "God help me!" she whispered. "I must get to Hyde Park before dawn breaks! Piers' life could depend on it!"

Elizabeth was sound asleep.

Lucy snatched her cloak and hurrying downstairs, shook Carew awake.

"A horse, Miss Lucy, at this time?" he muttered sleepily. "Master Piers took the swiftest, but there is Bess."

"Then for God's sake saddle her quickly!" Lucy cried, and minutes later she rode out of Kempston House at a gallop. Thank heaven her mockery of a masquerade had at least taught her to ride!

She was unaware of the fine drizzle and the wind as she raced through London, and of the mud from the horse's hooves that spattered her gown. The only thought in her mind was to get to the Ring in time to avert the duel.

Houses, trees, fields slipped by, until at last Hyde Park came in sight. She looked hastily for a gateway in the deer-palings that enclosed it. The sky was light towards the east now – pray God she would be in time!

The gateway – she galloped through and headed north to where Elizabeth had said the Ring lay. To her vexation several pools of water lay in her way, and deer were already lapping gently. She circumvented the pools with some difficulty, becoming even more mud-spattered as she did so, until a large copse of trees was before her. This must be where the Ring lay!

She spurred Bess on, foam-flecked and steaming as the poor jade was, and soon above the thunder of her hooves she could hear the clash of steel. The duel had begun! Lucy's heart thundered with the hooves. At least both contestants must still be alive!

She rounded the trees. In the mist two figures, sword in hand, circled each other warily, and she could see Toby and another man under the trees, watching. She leapt down from her horse.

"Stop, for God's sake, stop!" she cried. "There has been a dreadful mistake!"

Neither swordsman looked up at her; each was too wary of the other.

"Lucy, what are you doing here?" Toby demanded sharply. "This is no place for a woman. Go back at once to Kempston House."

"Toby, you must stop them!" Lucy cried, clutching his sleeve in supplication. His eyes were unswervingly on the duellists as he answered.

"In a matter of honour such as this, the affair cannot end until one or other defeats his opponent. How did you come to know of this?" he added, still watching the men closely. A crash of steel on steel rang out, and Toby gasped. The Count was pressing home his advantage over Piers, who was backing up against a tree.

Lucy threw back her hood and ran between the duellists.

"Come back, you fool!" Toby cried.

Lucy flung up her arms. "Piers, stop! Count Reichendorf, it is I!"

"Stand aside!" Piers barked. The Count's eyes flickered to Lucy and back to Piers. "I regret I am rather occupied at this moment, Elizabeth; later if you would permit."

"Elizabeth?" Piers murmured, still on guard.

"Let not her beauty distract you," sneered the Count. "We shall settle this business first, then the winner may enjoy her beauty as long as he will later." He flicked his sword point dangerously close to Piers' face.

"Elizabeth?" Piers murmured again, but louder this time.

"That is what I am trying to tell you," Lucy cried. "The Count believes me to be Elizabeth!"

Piers' eyes widened as understanding came. The Count's eyes narrowed in perplexity. He lowered his sword slowly and stepped back.

"Let us call a halt a moment, Herr Armytage," he said. "I do not understand. This is the lady of whom I spoke, the Lady Elizabeth. Do I understand we were not speaking of the same person?"

Piers was smiling broadly now. Toby and the other second hurried forward.

"There has indeed been a misunderstanding," Piers said to the Count. "Put up your sword, I pray. This is not Elizabeth, Lady Sherdley."

"Then who are you?" the Count asked, turning to Lucy.

"My name is Lucy Howe," she answered quietly. "I am Lady Elizabeth's companion." She turned to Piers. "I can never forgive myself. Because of my masquerade you could have lost your life," she said humbly, looking down at the wet grass beneath the

175

oak tree. "Piers, can you ever forgive me?"

When there was no answer, Lucy looked up. Piers was leaning against the tree trunk, his forehead against his arm. Lucy felt sick with apprehension at the explosion she was sure would follow.

It was not Piers, however, but the Count who exploded with anger. "You are not, then, a lady of rank and wealth, as I took you for?" Lucy shook her head.

His face went white with rage, the scar showing red now. "You – cheat, you liar!" he fumed.

"As I told you sir, I am Lady Elizabeth's maid and companion," she repeated. "I am sorry – deeply sorry – that my pretence has led you both to misconstrue and come so near to tragedy."

She had a sound like someone chuckling, and turned from the Count to Piers, who was still leaning against the tree, silently convulsed with laughter. Toby and the Count stood mystified.

"You find the deception amusing, Herr Armytage?" the Count said stiffly. "I assure you I do not ... I resent being duped by this – woman."

Piers laughed aloud. "Minutes ago you would have risked your life for this 'woman'," he said. "You spent much time urging your 'prior claim' on her, remember?"

The Count's face flushed. He turned away to take his cloak from his second, then he turned again to Piers.

"I regret the misunderstanding, sir," he said frostily, "and would ask your forgiveness for any slight upon your wife's honour."

"I forgive you, in view of the circumstances," Piers replied, "but now I can tell you that the Lady Elizabeth is not my wife but my sister-in-law."

"Then why did you let me believe you were her husband?" the Count asked.

Piers eyes him a moment. "My brother is somewhat older and less athletic than you, and when you had the presumption to enter Kempston House and demand 'my wife' from me, I let you continue in your mistake."

"Ah yes, I jumped to this conclusion because you came to Paris for her," the Count murmured.

Piers started to laugh softly again.

"You laugh?" snapped the Count. "Why?"

"Your fascinating maid is free now – little Lucy, the tavern wench from Southwark –

will you not press your 'prior claim' and take her with you?"

"Tavern wench?" The Count turned sharply and looked at Lucy. "Mein Gott!" His lips set in a hard line with disgust, then he strode away with his second to where the horses stood tethered.

Piers' chuckle turned to hilarious laughter in which Toby joined with noisy enjoyment as the Count galloped away. The two men laughed till the tears ran, and clutched each other's shoulders for support as they became weak from laughing.

Lucy's cheeks burned with shame and embarrassment. Relief at Piers' safety began to fade as the men laughed themselves to a standstill. In its place anger began to smoulder, anger that they should mock her so.

Piers wiped the tears from his eyes and turned to her.

"I am glad you came when you did," he said to her, still smiling mockingly. "The Count's reputation as a swordsman is renowned, and I was greatly at a disadvantage. For Elizabeth's honour I would risk all, but..." he broke off, and the chuckle began again.

Lucy's rage burst its floodgates. She leapt on to Bess, her cheeks blazing, and raced back to Kempston House. How she hated that cruel, mocking man! How he despised her! For Elizabeth he would fight, but for her, a tavern wench, it was laughable even to consider it!

And he had admitted the Count's 'prior claim' too. He truly believed that she had surrendered herself to that cold-blooded, avaricious Count. How despicable could a man become?

Lucy's mind was now made up irrevocably. She would leave Kempston House today.

CHAPTER 14

Lucy did not bid Elizabeth farewell before she left. She took nothing with her apart from the worsted gown and shoes and cloak she had been given on first arriving there.

The drizzle of the morning persisted all day, and the wind blew even more strongly. As Lucy left the city and crossed London Bridge into Southwark, she stopped to lean over the railings and survey the river. Not a boat had put out, but sought shelter instead at the banks. One had broken loose from its moorings and was being carried downstream towards the bridge, where the waters swirled and eddied in their fight to get through the nineteen small arches of the bridge.

Lucy stepped back from the railings when she felt them trembling in the wind. It was a day to suit her mood, she reflected, grey, turbulent and restless. The wind whipped her gown tightly about her thighs and her cloak flapped wildly behind her. Once amongst the tight-packed houses of South-wark, however, she was protected from the wind's fierceness.

She hastened towards Butcher's Row. Thomas and Piers had both said Molly was no longer there, but it was possible she might have returned there once the threat of plague had passed.

There were several red-crossed houses in the Row, but no mark on Molly's door. No answer came to Lucy's knock. She opened the door and went in. When her eyes grew accustomed to the gloom it became appar-ent that neither Molly nor anyone else was living there. Molly was never fanatic about keeping the room clean, but now its brick floor was knee-deep in litter that had blown in under the ill-fitting door, and the ceiling was festooned with cobwebs. The remains of Molly's straw mattress lay strewn around the floor, rats having apparently devoured the rest.

"Lookin' for someone?" a voice asked.

Lucy turned. A gaunt, hollow-eyed woman with a tattered shawl stood in the doorway.

"Molly Howe," Lucy said eagerly. "Do you know where I might find her?"

"Don't know anyone of that name," the

woman replied. "I been 'ere in the Row six months and never knew anyone of that name."

"Thank you," said Lucy. So it would seem Molly had gone by last August – when the plague was at its height, she mused as she walked towards the Tabard. She shuddered at the picture her fertile imagination conjured up – Molly, alone and dying of the plague, unable to call for help, or ignored by terror-mad passers-by, finally succumbing and lying dead and unburied until the rats finally removed the last traces of her.

She pushed the horrific picture out of her mind and quickened her steps. Trade was slack at the Tabard; in fact not a customer was to be seen. Life in the city was near enough normal again, but in the poorer districts citizens were reluctant to return while a few cases of plague still lingered. Garth, as large and slow-moving as ever, was sweeping the floor with his besom.

"Lucy lass!" he said gently, laying aside his broom and opening his arms to her. Lucy ran to him, and buried her face in his rough-shirted chest. She would have wept in his comforting arms but finding Molly was more imperative. She looked up at his genial, plump face.

"Molly – where is she, Garth? I must find her."

"Molly? That I cannot tell, Lucy love," he said, the folds between his chins deepening. "It's been many a week since she was here."

"Many a week?" repeated Lucy, a quiver of hope in her voice. "Then she's been here during the last six months?"

"Aye lass, but it were many weeks ago the last time she was in."

"How was she, Garth? Was she well?"

"Well enough. She escaped the sickness, but there was naught to be had to eat, and she was losing some of her plump charms," Garth smiled. "Do not fret yourself, Lucy, she has had to care for herself many a year and is well able to do so yet, if I know aught of Molly Howe. And what of you, Lucy? You were spared the sickness?"

Lucy brushed the question aside. "I was abroad, out of harm's way. But you survived – and your wife? Did you stay here?" Lucy was suddenly aware that Mistress Garth was not about and there was no succulent smell of cooking coming from the kitchen.

"May the Lord have mercy on her soul," said Garth sadly. "We stayed here, more's the pity, for my wife was taken by the sickness last September. I should have insisted on her going down to stay with my sister at Rochester."

"Oh Garth!" Lucy cried, "my poor Garth!"

"'T was a terrible sight, Lucy lass. Thank God you were spared that! You cannot imagine it. Everywhere around us people were dying, but when it came to my Prue – oh! the agony she suffered with those swellings! At the end it drove her out of her mind. She wanted to burn those great hard lumps off, or cut them, so much in pain she was, and when I stayed her hand, she made to throw herself in the river.

"She died in my arms, raving mad, Lucy – my Prue, who never raised her voice in her life." There was a catch in Garth's voice. "Forgive me, lass. I've not spoken of this to anyone till now. You was always like our own," he said, putting his arm across her shoulders.

"Do you want me to come back to work for you?" Lucy asked impulsively.

Garth shook his head slowly. "There's very few who come in to eat or sup these days," he said. "Come the fine weather perchance they'll be back, but we shall see. Till then I have little enough to do, and no money coming in to pay for help."

"Let me go and look for Molly, and when I find her I'll come to you again," Lucy said. "Money I shall not want from you; you have done enough for me already."

"Nay, lass," replied Garth slowly, "if trade don't pick up I shall probably go and live with my sister."

He watched her hurry away again, but she paused out in the street. She had no idea where to begin looking now, and still the wind whistled round every corner, though the rain was clearing. For hours she searched every alley and street. Very few folk were about, and she recognised none of them.

At last night fell. Hungry and exhausted, Lucy crawled back to Molly's house in Butcher's Row where at least she might sleep protected from the weather.

She awoke ravenously hungry. For the first time in almost a year, Lucy knew real hunger once again. Forcing it out of her mind, again she walked all day, searching every inn and tavern this side of the river, where Molly might go in search of clients. Again she met with no success.

Garth had spoken of the pest fields, the massive communal pits dug for those dead of the plague; one lay at Tothill Fields, she knew, and no doubt she could find others too, but to what purpose? The spots were unmarked and unnamed; even parish registers had been hard put to it to list the names of all who perished. In their panic, many had fled from one parish to another or even out of London, so how could one trace the movements of one person alone?

In the evening the wind dropped and a mist began to form. By the time Lucy reached the river bank it had became a soupy fog, ominously silent save for the plash of water. Night and fog were a wicked combination in London, rendering a harmless citizen easy prey for robbers or for the river itself. Lucy picked her way with care, growing more apprehensive with each step.

The distant throb of a drum cut into the silent air. Lucy knew this was to guide the wherrymen still afloat safely to shore, but the sound was sinister and frightening in this vast brown vacuum. She drew her hood across her face in an effort to keep the filthy vapour out of her nostrils.

It was useless, she decided. She would have to abandon the search until daylight.

Suddenly out of the mist the figure of a man appeared. Lucy cried out involuntarily before she recognised the tall, striding figure of Edgar, the pedlar who shammed his wounded soldier act to squeeze money from gullible passers-by.

"Edgar!"

"By my troth, Lucy Howe!" he exclaimed.

"Oh, Edgar, have you seen Molly lately? I've been looking for her everywhere, but no-one knows where she is. Can you tell me?"

She looked anxiously into his weather-beaten face. Edgar's welcoming smile had faded as she spoke. There was a long silence, broken only by the throb of the drums, before he put his hands on her shoulders.

"Search no more, lass. Go home to your friends and leave it be. 'T will be for the best," he said kindly.

"But I must find her, Edgar, I promised..."

"It's too late, Lucy. Get you home."

"Too late?" Lucy's voice quivered in apprehension. "Why, Edgar?" Edgar shook his head sadly and looked away. "Tell me – you must tell me! Something has befallen her, has it not, and you do not wish to hurt me. But I *must* know!"

Edgar looked directly into her eyes. "She's gone, lass. She's dead. And there's an end to it."

"But how? Was it the plague?"

He shook his head. "Nay, she survived that."

"Then what?"

" 'T was the river."

Lucy was dumbstruck. The river? Molly was not the sort to take her own life, no matter how desperate she was. An accident then? Dimly, through her confused thoughts, Lucy heard Edgar speaking again.

"No-one knows how she came to be there. I only know that my Betsy told me she'd seen a woman fished out of the river, and she thought it was Molly."

"Thought it was? Then it is possible..." Lucy began, a flicker of hope in her voice.

"No, lass. It was Molly right enough," Edgar cut in. "I went down to the deadhouse to see for myself."

Lucy shuddered at the thought of the deadhouse, a long, low building on the shores of the river, with a single huge oak door studded with iron nails. It was a grim place where corpses fished out of the river were taken for identification before burial, and always a foetid evil smell hung about the place. What a foul spot for Molly to end her days! Again Lucy felt conscience-stricken at her own neglect. Edgar cut short her morbid thoughts.

188

"No point in dwelling on it, lass," he said curtly, but Lucy knew his abruptness was only an attempt to conceal the concern he felt for her. "She's gone, no matter which way, and that means she's seen the last of suffering. No-one can hurt her now, lass, so you've no need to fret yourself on her behalf."

Lucy nodded dumbly, but Edgar's words could not ease the ache in her heart.

"Come, Lucy," he said. "I'll see you back to London Bridge. You'll never find your way in this filthy stuff," and he drew her arm though his. She was glad of the warm strength of his arm and stupidly, as in a nightmare, she stumbled along beside him.

At the Southwark end of the bridge Edgar halted. "Remember lass, Molly's life was never an easy one. She's well out of it now, so go you home to your friends and make your own life as she would have wished. Goodnight, Lucy, and God be with you."

He turned and hurried away into the swirling fog. Lucy's mind was a turmoil of grief and guilt as she crossed back over the bridge that separated her old way of life from the new.

CHAPTER 15

Dazed and sick at heart, Lucy found herself next morning back in Kempston House. She was unaware of having walked there or how she got there. Her throat ached with unshed tears, and she was grateful to see a warm, friendly face.

Elizabeth closed the ledger in which she had been entering her household accounts. "Lucy, my dear! I have been so worried for you in this foul weather. I am happy to see you back, for two days is an eternity without you," she cried, throwing her arms about Lucy's shoulders.

She looked better than when Lucy left; her pallor had faded and there was a happy light in her eyes. The light waned when Lucy, touched by her unselfish warmth, broke down and sobbed. The agony of the last two days broke loose. When she recounted the details of Molly's death, Elizabeth wept too.

Jennet came in, round-eyed with curiosity.

"Go to Mrs. Platt and ask her to send up some of the cold chicken and some bread and ale. Lucy must be starving," Elizabeth ordered, drying her eyes and composing herself. Jennet scuttled out.

"You shall stay with me always, Lucy. You shall never want for a home, fear not," Elizabeth smiled gently. "I am taking care of my own interests too, for my responsibilities will be enlarged by the autumn, and I shall have need of you ever more then."

Lucy dabbed her tears and regarded Elizabeth with curiosity. There was an unaccustomed sparkle in her eyes.

"Oh Lucy! I am so happy, it seems cruel in the face of your bitter grief. I had suspected it, but could not bring myself to believe it was true, for fear of tempting Providence. But today Thomas had his physician come to see me. Lucy, I am with child!"

Lucy gazed at Elizabeth in surprise. With her fragile, golden beauty and ecstatic smile she seemed no more than a child herself. There was no doubt she was deliriously happy to be bearing her beloved Thomas a child. For anyone else but Elizabeth Lucy would have felt unbridled envy but for Elizabeth, whose prime concern was the happiness of others and who doted on

191

children, she could feel only gladness and gratitude.

She took Elizabeth's hands in her own. "I am so happy for you, Elizabeth, truly I am. When is it to be?"

"The end of September. Is it not wonderful?" Elizabeth replied. She paused then looked sadly at Lucy. "For every death there is a birth, they say. I hope you may take some little crumb of comfort from that, Lucy."

Jennet returned with the tray of food. Lucy, though ravenous, felt she had little appetite but ate to please Elizabeth, who then persuaded her to go and rest for a while.

But sleep would not come to Lucy. She was still tormented over Molly, whom she had loved and left, and who had been reduced to such abject misery that the river had become her destiny. Lucy's heart ached. Was the river an accidental end, was it Molly's solution to an impossible life, or was she driven made like so many others in this dreadful year?

Whatever the reason, Lucy knew she would never overcome the feeling of guilt, that she had not been there to help. Guilt too was on her conscience over Elizabeth and the masquerade to Count Reichendorf. In her numbness over Molly, Lucy had completely forgotten him, and Piers' mockery and laughter when he found out. How could she face Piers again after that? He was so cruelly, tauntingly amused at the hoax which had so nearly had tragic consequences. Would he allow her to remain in Kempston House? And if not, how could she explain to Elizabeth without telling her of the Count? Elizabeth would feel terribly let down, to be deserted before she gave birth to her child.

Next day Lucy met Piers in the corridor, their first meeting since the day of the duel. Her heart turned over when she saw his tall dark figure approaching and she felt a flutter of apprehension.

"I wish to speak to you, Lucy," he announced quietly. "Come into my studio."

It was the first time she had been allowed in his studio. Everywhere there were canvases and oils, water colours and brushes. Finished paintings stood propped against the walls, and one still stood, covered by hessian, on the easel. That would no doubt be the portrait of Rebecca he was still working on, she reflected.

Piers was gazing out of the window, his

back towards her. There was a suppressed power and virility in the breadth of his shoulders that gave him an air of masculine protectiveness. Lucy waited for him to speak. Finally he turned.

"You must be aware that since your coming here you have created nothing but trouble," he said, his face set and expressionless. Lucy bit her lip and looked at the floor. "You have deliberately incensed my cousin and flouted her authority, you have taken liberties far above those reasonably to be expected by a servant, and finally you have contrived such an act of duplicity as to bring my sister-in-law's honour into question."

Lucy looked up quickly, her face glowing with shame. She opened her mouth to defend herself, but he saw her intention.

"No, do not offer to defend or explain your actions. I understand now why you were so anxious to speak to me after the Count's visit. I appreciate that you would probably have confessed in order to protect Elizabeth, but that is not sufficient."

"Then what would you have had me do?" she cried angrily.

"You should never have posed as Elizabeth in the first place. It was your ambition, it would seem, that led you to ape the lady. But if you had to impersonate her, you might at least have conducted yourself like a lady, and not like a tavern trollop. You saw what your duplicity led to; Elizabeth's honour brought into question could have caused dreadful suffering both to her and to Thomas."

Piers' voice was icy. Lucy cut in, "Neither Elizabeth nor Thomas know of this, then?"

"No," he answered curtly, and turned and looked out of the window again.

"Thank you," Lucy murmured.

"Do not thank me," Piers replied, his back still towards her. "It was not out of concern for your feelings; I did not wish to hurt them, and as Count Reichendorf fortunately took me for Elizabeth's husband, it was not necessary to tell Thomas. You will, no doubt, be glad to hear that the Count has left England, so you are safe now."

Safe from exposure, did he mean, or from the Count? Not the latter, surely; the Count's obvious disgust when he discovered Lucy to be a tavern maid would not lead anyone to suppose that he would pursue her any further.

"In view of the trouble and danger you have caused, therefore, I consider it would be best if you left here," Piers continued slowly. Obviously he had not even been aware of her absence during the last two days.

"I cannot leave now," she cried. "Elizabeth is with child and wants me with her!"

Piers turned, astonishment in his eyes. "So soon?" he murmured. "You see now how the Count could have substantiated his claim over her, had he so wished."

He paused.

"I beg your pardon, Piers," Rebecca's voice cut in sweetly. She was standing in the doorway, the deep rich red of her velvet gown giving vivid emphasis to her raven hair and milky skin. "You asked me to sit for you this afternoon," she reminded him.

Lucy knew the sweetness of her smile was feigned, no doubt because she had overheard Piers bidding Lucy to leave Kempston House.

"You may go," Piers said to Lucy, and went to arrange the chair for Rebecca. As she swept by Lucy, ignoring her, Lucy could not but notice the brightness of her eye. It was the look of a woman in love.

All that evening Lucy's brain raced as she busied herself with Elizabeth's wardrobe. Piers wanted her gone; Elizabeth needed her to stay. And Rebecca obviously would prefer Lucy's absence. Piers either did not know or did not care about Molly's death, that he was so harsh as to dismiss her now, with no place to shelter.

But Piers was not her master. It was not for him to decide whether she was to be dismissed. In any event, why should he set himself up as her judge, when his own actions had not always appeared strictly honourable? Again the image of Piers' face in the glow from the blazing letter flashed into her mind.

No, damn him, she would not just quietly disappear as he would wish. She would face him outright, challenge him about the letter, and refuse to leave Kempston House until either Elizabeth or Thomas, her rightful employers, asked her to go. It was unlikely he would force their hand by revealing the fact that Lucy's behaviour had led to the duel with the Count, for had he not said he wished to spare them?

Lucy waited until Elizabeth was soundly sleeping, then tiptoed along the corridor. Piers' voice was still to be heard in conversation in the study. She slipped into his studio and, closing the door quietly behind her, waited in the darkness for him to come up.

After some time she heard Piers' voice coming closer.

"Then it's all settled, Rebecca," she heard him say as the footsteps paused outside the door. "The marriage dowry Thomas is to settle on you is a handsome one indeed and should ensure a rare degree of comfort. I think it would be best if the wedding were to take place after Elizabeth's confinement is safely over, say in October or November. Will that please you? Can you be patient for six months?"

"Indeed it will, Piers," Rebecca's voice held a warm softness in place of its usual grating harshness. There was a moment's silence outside the door, then the sound of a kiss.

"Goodnight then, Becky."

"Goodnight, Piers."

Rebecca's footsteps faded and the door opened. Lucy was horror-struck. Piers would be furious to know she had overheard what were presumably private family plans. Before Piers could light the candles she had slipped behind the heavy velvet hangings of the window and stood there, tense, hardly daring to breathe.

Through a crack she saw Piers unbutton

his doublet and throw it carelessly over a chest, then throw back the hessian covering the painting that stood on the easel. He stood contemplating it a moment, stroking his chin thoughtfully, then uttered a sigh of contentment.

Lucy felt bitter jealously welling up inside her. It was undoubtedly the new portrait of Rebecca he was regarding with such frank admiration. After a moment he took the candle in his hand and went through the connecting door to his chamber.

Darkness fell again in the studio. Lucy hesitantly opened the curtains wider, and slipped through. A shaft of moonlight through the aperture fell athwart the canvas and as Lucy passed it she gave a sudden start. It was not Rebecca's proud flamboyant beauty that stared at her from the easel, but her own face!

She stopped and gazed at it, mesmerised. Why should Piers be painting her portrait? She looked closer. In the moonlight the head had a defiant tilt to it, and the mouth and eyes a hard mocking look. The hair was not decorously looped or ringletted, but falling in a riotous confusion of red curls across one bare shoulder.

A feeling Lucy recognised well began to

surge up from the pit of her stomach towards her throat. How dare he!

She glared at the door of his chamber. For a second she was about to burst in and demand of him, why the devil he should portray her thus. Just because he hated and despised her was no justification for this, for handing her down to posterity as a cheap, tawdry slut.

Then reason prevailed. To be heard storming in Piers' chamber after midnight would indeed by misconstrued. It would serve him aright if Rebecca misunderstood and broke of their betrothal, Lucy thought vindictively. Then she realised, it was not such anger she felt, as hurt and betrayal. Whatever she did seemed doomed to be misunderstood.

Quietly she turned the handle of the door to the corridor; at the same instant the connecting door to Piers' chamber opened. He stood there, the candle aloft.

"Ah Lucy," he said, and the vibrant voice sent a shiver through her. He did not seem surprised to see her there. "I had hoped to see you this evening. I was hasty in what I said. I did not know Elizabeth was with child until you told me. That being so, I understand her wishing to keep you here."

Why must he sound so kindly and

understanding, Lucy raged inwardly. Had he still been angry, I could have taxed him with the King's letter.

He came to stand near her, by the open door.

"Elizabeth finds you the most congenial of souls; there is between you a kind of rapport which unfortunately does not exist between her and Rebecca," he went on quietly. "In the circumstances it would be best if you were to stay by her until she is safely delivered.

"I must warn you, however, that your presence in this house is profoundly disturbing, and I should be grateful if you would keep out of sight as far as possible," he went on.

"Who finds me so disturbing?" Lucy demanded angrily.

He looked at her intently. "To my cousin you are, as you are well aware, a constant source of irritation."

"And to you? Thomas and Elizabeth do not regard me thus, just Rebecca and you. Admit it, you despise me too, do you not?" Lucy flared.

"Keep your voice low, mistress," Piers said curtly. "Do you wish to awaken the household?"

"Admit it then, Master Piers," Lucy

mocked him.

There was a pause.

"Very well, mistress Lucy. I admit I find your presence disturbing, and would be obliged if, while we are to stay under the same roof, you would be so kind as to keep out of my way."

Without another word he re-entered the studio and closed the door firmly behind him.

CHAPTER 16

It was not difficult for Lucy to keep out of Piers' way for the next few weeks, for Elizabeth claimed all her attention. Thomas's radiance at the knowledge that he was to become a father soon gave way to concern for Elizabeth, for she was sick every morning.

Lucy felt desperately sorry for her, pale and prostrate from the time she rose each morning until midday. Eventually Elizabeth was persuaded to stay abed late, though she was very reluctant to do so.

"The physician says there is naught amiss with me, this is a symptom only to be expected, and perfectly normal," she said weakly. "I feel ashamed to lie abed when I should be directing the affairs of my household."

"Soon, Elizabeth, not yet," Lucy replied soothingly. " 'T will pass, and then you can

203

resume your duties. In the meantime, I am sure Rebecca will manage capably."

If she has a mind for aught else but her marriage, Lucy thought privately. Rebecca was a changed woman of late; there was a softer, kinder air about her, and the atmosphere in the house more kindly-disposed than Lucy had ever known it before. Jennet came in for fewer beatings than hitherto, and judging by her bewildered little face, she could not account for her good fortune.

Lucy could not care for Elizabeth devotedly enough to appease her conscience. Still she was haunted by nightmares from time to time of her own thoughtless behaviour with Count Reichendorf which had so nearly led to disgrace for Elizabeth, but for Piers' timely action. And haunted by dreams too of Molly's hideous death. Whether Molly had been driven to drown herself, or whether it was an accident, worried Lucy. If Molly had been driven to suicide, what was the reason, and could Lucy have prevented it?

Her concern for Elizabeth and the physical effort involved in nursing her afforded Lucy little time for brooding, and gradually the nightmares diminished and died.

Spring came again to London, and with it

the hope of a happier year now the dreadful year of plague was over. Piers and Rebecca were happy, Lucy could see, setting off to go riding in the Park with Toby, or laughing together in Piers' studio while he painted.

Were they laughing at that cruel portrait of herself, Lucy wondered, or simply happy together, Rebecca posing while Piers continued painting her? Lucy wished she had seen his picture of Rebecca that night she had been in his studio, but she had been so thunderstruck by the image of herself, caught in the shaft of moonlight, that she had eyes for naught else.

She listened avidly to the gossip in the kitchen, but Mrs. Platt and Carew and the others seemed to have caught no whisper of impending marriage in the family. Their main topic of conversation was Elizabeth's expected child.

"Poor chuck," Mrs. Platt would say. "She'll have a harder time of it than most, I'll be bound, so slender and fragile she is."

"Not she!" snorted old Mother Benson, "Not with me there to help her. I delivered his mother of Master Piers single-handed, and she was very bit as tiny as my lady Elizabeth, and him a great lump of a lad."

Mother Benson was enjoying her renewed

importance in the household. Since Piers' childhood there had been no more babies for her to care for in Kempston House, and she was looking forward eagerly to the new arrival.

"Lovely babe, 'e was," she went on, her eyes soft and tender as she looked back through the years. "Fine, strapping lad, unlike Master Thomas. I delivered him too," she added proudly, "and they said he would not live, and Mistress Armytage would never be able to bear another child. But when she conceived of Master Piers, many years later, it was a miracle, they said. And look at 'im now, 'andsomest man in London. Make a fine 'usband for some lucky girl, 'e will."

For Rebecca, Lucy thought bitterly. The group around the deal table nodded deferentially to Mother Benson. She might have delivered only two babes in her life, but against the odds they had both survived, and that was no mean achievement for the times.

A pale yellow spring of daffodils and heavy-scented lilacs mellowed into a glorious golden summer. Elizabeth grew strong again and resumed her tasks as mistress of Kempston House. Her joyous air of anticipation gave Lucy a deep inner satisfaction; she was making some atonement to Elizabeth in taking care of her.

Piers no longer turned brusquely aside when he saw Lucy approaching, but instead gave her a slow smile as he passed. He is content with life, Lucy thought, and can afford to look with pleasure upon even me, a creature he loathed hitherto. Whatever the reason, she was content enough, and basked in his approval.

Thomas made his concern for Elizabeth's comfort apparent.

"Would you like to have your mother, Lady Catherine, come for her much-delayed visit now, my dear?" he asked her, his grey eyes scanning her pale face. "Or would you prefer her to come later, to Longacre, when your birthing is imminent?"

Elizabeth clasped her hands in pleasure. "Oh now, Thomas, if you please. It is so long since we met, and I have so much to tell her. She would be so happy to see how content I am now, for you know how anxious she was."

"To be sure, my dear. And she may come again to Longacre, as soon as she wishes, to see her grandchild."

Piers was no less concerned. When Lady

Catherine wrote to say she would be happy to come at once, Piers set off on the long journey north to escort her.

To Lucy, despite the flurry of activity in preparation for the visit, the house seemed achingly empty in Piers' absence. She felt irritated with herself. Why should Piers, absent or present, concern her so much? He did not care for her, a foolish servant, and she could not care for a man she knew to be treacherous, and moreover, soon to be married.

She busied herself helping Elizabeth to sew tiny garments. "I shall sew all my babe's garments myself," Elizabeth declared. "I do not wish them to be sewn by the seamstress."

It was June, and the air was warm and scent-laden the day Lady Catherine and Piers were due to arrive at Kempston House. Elizabeth hurried up and down despite her increasing bulk, her eyes ashine with anticipation.

"Are you sure there are flowers in my mother's room? Roses are her favourite – I must go and see, and arrange them myself," she said, shaking off Thomas's restraining arm. Thomas looked appealingly at Lucy, who hurried out after Elizabeth.

At last the coach clattered into the yard. Lucy prevented Elizabeth from hurling herself headlong down the steps in delight, then stood back unobtrusively to watch. Piers' broad shoulders inclined as he lowered the step, then straightened to hold the hand of the lady about to alight. Lady Catherine was white-haired and birdlike, keen, lively eyes darting to the group on the steps and lighting up when she beheld Elizabeth.

She tripped across to the group with surprising agility and folded her arms about Elizabeth, murmuring gently in her ear. Lucy saw tears brimming in Elizabeth's eyes as they turned to enter the house, and deemed this a suitable moment to leave mother and daughter alone together for a time.

She looked up as she turned on the step, and met Piers' eyes, dark and thoughtful as he watched her.

"Elizabeth looks well," he commented. "You are tending her well, Lucy. We are grateful to you." He observed her closely a moment, and Lucy could not withstand the searching look. She lowered her gaze.

"Whatever your faults, your fondness for Elizabeth is your saving grace," he said. "I truly believe you meant it when you once said you would go through fire and water for her."

"So I would," Lucy responded quickly.

He smiled and entered the house. Lucy could hardly quell the fluttering in her breast aroused by those piercing black eyes. She hurried away to see to the unpacking of the trunks which Carew was staggering to carry up the stairs.

In the succeeding days it was evident to Lucy that Lady Catherine was well pleased with her daughter's new mode of life. Her keen blue eyes seemed to watch and register every movement of every member of the household. She reminded Lucy of a robin with her small, wiry build, her quick, deft movements and those alert, enquiring eyes.

One evening in the parlour when Piers was singing while Elizabeth played the virginals, Lucy became aware of Lady Catherine's quizzical gaze. She looked up into the intent blue eyes, then quickly away again. She flushed, conscious that the effect of Piers' strong, clear voice on her had probably been apparent in her face.

"Belle, qui tient ma vie," he sang, and although Lucy's French was not adequate to understand the whole of the meaning of the song, it was clear it was a love song.

Rebecca sat enraptured, her small, white teeth gleaming in the candlelight as she smiled. Toby sat, sprawling in a relaxed fashion in a chair beside Rebecca, and Thomas sat upright, enchanted, with eyes only for his beautiful wife.

Lucy and Lady Catherine sat on the fringe of the circle, and Lucy wished Lady Catherine would study another instead of herself. She had been so captivated by Piers' singing, even if the love song was directed at Rebecca, and now she felt uncomfortable.

She withdrew, murmuring an excuse to Lady Catherine about preparing Elizabeth's bed and night attire. No sooner had she reached Elizabeth's chamber, however, than the door opened again and Lady Catherine entered.

"A fine voice, n'est-ce pas?" she said, settling herself on the window seat to watch Lucy, "and a lovely song. Do you know it?" She cocked her head on one side, making the likeness to a robin even more striking.

"No, my lady. I know only that it was a French love song," Lucy replied, "and indeed it is beautiful."

"Like all love songs, it is best sung by one who is in love," said the old lady drily, "and Master Piers is very obviously in love."

Lucy felt a stab of jealousy. It would seem Lady Catherine had not yet been told of Piers' and Rebecca's betrothal. The family must have decided to keep it a secret so as not to detract from Elizabeth's glorious hour.

"I am happy to see my daughter is so well content," Lady Catherine continued. "I understand from her that you are her greatest friend." In the earnest blue eyes Lucy could see a striking resemblance to Elizabeth. "It was a gamble, sending my child to London life, but God was good; all has turned out well. She could want no kindlier husband, and she assures me of your loyal friendship. So before I return to Northumberland, I would entreat you to watch out for her still, Lucy. She is a stranger to the ways of the world, but I can see you have experienced much and have the strength and will to persevere in difficulties where she might falter. And the more so, now she is with child.

"Come here," she went on, patting the seat beside her. Lucy crossed and stood before her. "Sit by me." Lucy did so. The old lady leaned across and took Lucy's hands in her own.

"Promise me one thing," she said quietly.

"Though Elizabeth has not spoken of it, I can see there is no loss of affection between her and Rebecca. When the time comes, Elizabeth will be in sore need of a friend in her labour for this child. I shall not be here, so I entrust her to you. Do not leave her side for a second, I beg you."

Lucy looked into the lined but still handsome face smiling gently.

"I promise," she said simply. The old lady patted her hands in gratitude.

Lucy rose and began turning down the covers on the bed as Elizabeth came in, humming to herself happily.

"Is not that a beautiful song?" she asked, "and does not Piers sing it tenderly?"

"Indeed," said Lady Catherine, smiling fondly at her daughter. "Tell me, my French is a little rusty these days, how would you translate it, Elizabeth?"

"Belle qui tient ma vie? Oh, something like this, I should think:
Beauteous creature, who holds my life enchained
A prisoner to your eyes,
You have ravished my soul
With your glorious smile.
If only to appease my pain,
Come, my love, embrace me."

"Excellent!" said Lady Catherine. "A splendid translation! And a very meaningful message, for those who have ears to hear it."

"How do you mean, mama?" asked Elizabeth, but her eyes were on the tiny gown she had just finished sewing that afternoon, turning it over and admiring the tiny bows of lace on it.

"A love song, my dear, a message from Piers to a woman," Lady Catherine explained.

Lucy turned sharply from the press where she was selecting Elizabeth's nightgown, and surveyed Lady Catherine's face. Elizabeth was still deep in her own thoughts, but Lady Catherine's intent blue eyes were piercing deeply into Lucy's own.

"Piers is in love, deeply in love," she said in a low voice, "and could not take his eyes off the lady in question the whole time he was singing."

Lucy's face burned with surprised embarrassment and pain when she saw Lady Catherine nodding knowingly at her. Piers loves her! Impossible! In any case, he was to marry Rebecca, she wanted to cry out. But her soul longed to believe it, to take the soothing balm that he did not despise her. But love her? No, Lady Catherine was unfortunately mistaken.

But that did not prevent Lucy from crying herself to sleep that night with dreams of what might have been.

CHAPTER 17

Lady Catherine departed for Northumberland again after a month, content with Elizabeth's progress. The baby was now lively, kicking joyfully, and Elizabeth was radiant. She was able to bid her mother au revoir contentedly, promising to see her at Longacre in the autumn when she would have new evidence of her housewifely capabilities to show her.

July was hot and oppressive, and the air of London was rendered yet more ominous by the distant sound of gunfire. The Dutch and English fleets met and mangled each other in mid-Channel, and all London held its breath. At the end of the month the bells of London's churches rang to announce a decisive naval victory, and Londoners breathed freely once more. They were still masters of the sea.

King Charles had followed his wife to the salubrious waters of Tunbridge Wells, but

London was to celebrate the victory with a thanksgiving day nonetheless. The day chosen was also Lucy's birthday, August the fourteenth.

Toby arrived early at Kempston House, his eyes alight with the anticipation of a day's sport.

"There's to be bear-baiting, cock-fighting, fireworks and bonfires. Come now, Piers, who is to come with us? Rebecca, you will? Lucy?" He turned to Elizabeth, her head bent over her embroidery frame. "Elizabeth, I would fain take you and Thomas with us, but I fear your condition would not permit."

"No indeed," Elizabeth laughed. "Thomas and I prefer to remain at home, do we not, my dear?" She turned to Thomas. "But I am sure Rebecca and Lucy would enjoy the celebrations. Go, both of you, prepare."

And so Lucy found herself being ushered through the London streets alongside Rebecca, Piers and Toby either side of them. The air had that shimmer of heat and expectation that pinpoints every detail more acutely, and Lucy knew this was going to be a day to remember, whether Piers had planned on having her company or not. The atmosphere of subdued exultation seemed to communicate itself to her companions also, and Toby, Rebecca and Piers were all laughing and chattering merrily as they walked. Lucy felt happy, conscious she looked pretty in her jade green silk gown which set off her burnished hair. Rebecca looked ravishing in scarlet satin, with her black hair blowing in the breeze.

At midday people tumbled in droves out of the churches where they had been attending thanksgiving services, and they found themselves caught up in the lively, happy crowds pressing towards Bankside.

"That settles it," Piers laughed, "we must begin our day's sport at the Bear Garden, for the crowd will not suffer us to go in any other direction," and he and Toby bent their shoulders to the task of shielding the girls. Eventually they found themselves at the Bear Garden, but the sight of the bull tossing dogs about and the welter of blood bored Rebecca, who begged to move on.

The bear-baiting and the fights that frequently broke out between the spectators who had wagered heavily on them, was no more pleasing to the girls, so they all adjourned to a nearby inn for a meal of venison pasty and ale.

Then they took a boat up the river and the men sang lustily all the way to Spring

218

Gardens. There they walked and talked in the sunlight until evening fell, and then came back into town by river. All along the banks Lucy could see bonfires blazing, throwing flickering orange arcs against the night sky. Suddenly there was a shower of coloured sparks.

"Fireworks!" Rebecca breathed in ecstasy. "Oh Piers, Toby, let us go ashore and see them!"

Toby obligingly ordered the wherryman to tie up at the nearest stairs, then he and Piers helped the girls ashore. Rebecca giggled as the hem of her gown caught the water and splashed her ankles, then caught Piers by the hand.

"Come on!" she cried, running and tugging, and all three ran after her.

Around the bonfire a vast crowd heaved and pushed. Boys ran hither and thither throwing their rockets and sizzling serpents at each other and amongst the legs of the spectators who, in turn, shrieked and ran. Rebecca screamed happily as a serpent flashed about her feet and Toby swung her up in the air. Lucy fell back behind Piers, glad of his breadth to shield her. To her surprise, he gathered her inside his cloak, his arm about her shoulders.

"You are not afraid, Lucy?" he murmured.

"No!" she cried, then added more truthfully, "well, only a little."

He smiled and held her closer. His warmth suffused her body, causing her to tremble. She tried to beat down the rising joy inside her at his touch, then saw Rebecca's curious gaze upon them both. Instantly Lucy froze; her mounting excitement died away, and she stiffened.

Rebecca smiled coolly. " 'T is time we returned, I think, Piers. No doubt Elizabeth has had our supper kept ready for us."

Piers nodded in agreement and turned, still holding tightly on Lucy's shoulders. Toby drew Rebecca's arm through his own and she smiled up into his face. Lucy thought she had never seen Rebecca look lovelier than at this moment, with her creamy skin and dark eyes flashing in the firelight. It was no wonder Piers, and possibly Toby too, should fall in love with her.

The thought faded as Piers' closeness again was borne in on Lucy. His arm rested lightly on her shoulder, but now and again as he talked his fingers tightened on her upper arm, as though to give emphasis to his words, and each time Lucy thrilled to the pressure.

Nearing Kempston House, Piers suddenly said, "This has been a great day, has it not? I have enjoyed myself immensely, and I know Toby and Rebecca have also. I shall remember this as a day when we grew to know each other better. A special day, Lucy," he added in lower tones. "And for you?"

Lucy nodded, too happy for a moment to speak, then managed to murmur, "To be sure, Master Piers, it is a special day indeed for me. I shall always remember my eighteenth birthday. Thank you for a wonderful day."

"Your birthday?" Piers stopped in surprise and turned to face her. "You did not tell me it was your birthday. No-one knows?"

"Elizabeth knew. This morning she gave me a beautiful silk wrap trimmed with lace."

Piers frowned, his hand stroking his chin in a gesture Lucy recognised to be characteristic of the man. Rebecca and Toby passed them by, laughing at some private joke, and rang the bell for Carew. Then they stood on the steps, watching Piers and Lucy, but Piers seemed quite unaware of them.

"I am so sorry I did not know, Lucy, but if

you would permit me, I shall make you a gift of something that I treasure. In the meantime, would you allow me to salute you on your birthday?"

Lucy looked up at him uncomprehendingly. Slowly he bent his head and kissed her tenderly. Rebecca's laugh trilled out, and Lucy heard the doors open and the footsteps fade away inside. She felt Piers' arms close gently around her and fold her closely to him. Her whole body became one surge of emotion and she melted into his embrace, returning his kiss with equal fervour.

Then Piers slowly released her and stood back. "Many, many happy returns of your birthday, Lucy," he said quietly, and taking her hand, he led her indoors. Once inside, Lucy's bewildered faculties began to function once more. Piers had kissed her, and it was no light-hearted birthday greeting, of that she felt sure, but the passionate kiss of a man for a woman! Lucy's heart leapt with joy, until she remembered – he was betrothed to Rebecca, and was to marry her in the autumn.

She remembered Rebecca's shrill laugh out there on the doorstep, and shame flooded her body. Rebecca and Toby were waiting for them in the vestibule, and there was a cool, mocking smile on Rebecca's face.

Lucy tugged her hand free from Piers' and ran upstairs to her chamber. There she flung herself on the truckle bed and wept with abject shame and misery.

Now she knew for certain that, traitor or no, she loved Piers with her whole being. And there was nothing she could do about it. Lucy's primitive instincts told her to fight, but what would that achieve? She could not wrest him from Rebecca if he wished to marry his cousin. She could not leave Kempston House after her promises to Lady Catherine and to Piers himself to look after Elizabeth.

There was no alternative but to remain and do as he himself had earlier suggested – keep out of his way. She could see Elizabeth safely through her confinement, but she could not stay and see Piers and Rebecca wedded – that was too great a price to pay. Lucy's pride could not withstand that.

Elizabeth seemed quite unaware of Lucy's withdrawn subdued behaviour next morning. She was full of plans for the birth of her baby at Longacre, now only six weeks away.

"I have not yet seen Longacre, but from

Thomas's description it sounds a perfect place for an infant, Lucy. Set deep in the countryside, with huge gardens and an orchard, trees and shrubs, gravel paths, and even an aviary and some beehives. I shall be able to make my own herb garden as I had in Northumberland. Thomas is going to erect a sundial and have an orangery planted out. Does it not sound a healthy place to rear our children?"

Lucy murmured her agreement. "When do you intend to go to Longacre, Elizabeth?" she asked.

"Mid-September, I fancy," Elizabeth replied, "but Thomas and Rebecca are going down in a couple of weeks to ensure everything is in readiness for the birthing. They will take Mother Benson, who is to deliver me, and install her there in charge of the final arrangements. I have asked her to retrim the family cradle with fresh lace for our child." Elizabeth smiled tenderly in the way of all mothers near their time, her eyes full of anticipation and dreams for her child.

"I want only you and Mother Benson there when the babe is born," she said softly. "I would have Thomas too but it is still frowned upon for men to be present at a birthing, even of their own children, more's the pity. Still, it would probably only cause him distress not to be able to help me, so perhaps it is best."

There was a knock at Elizabeth's door, and Piers entered.

"How does my favourite sister-in-law fare this fine morning?" he smiled, then turned to Lucy. "I have come to borrow Lucy from you a moment. There is something I promised her yesterday that I would show her, if you will permit."

"Of course," said Elizabeth. "Away with you both."

Lucy followed Piers along the corridor, hoping he would not notice the flush on her cheeks. How could she cling to her determination to avoid him if he deliberately sought her company thus? It was very cruel and unfair. What could he want? Ah yes, the gift he had promised – something he treasured, he had said. What could that be?

Piers stopped outside his studio.

"I hope you will like this," he said. "If you find it has faults, pray remember I did the best I was capable of, and my merits as a painter are far from perfect, of that I am well aware."

The portrait! He was going to make her a gift of that horrible, cruel portrait of herself!

Lucy was beside herself with shame and anger. Not only to portray her thus but then to add insult to injury by expecting her to hang it and expose it to public view – that was too much!

In a fury of silent indignation she followed him inside. Piers crossed to the easel and took hold of the corner of the hessian that covered it.

"Stop!" Lucy cried.

Startled by the suddenness of her cry, Piers paused. He turned and looked at her, dark eyes wide and enquiring.

"What is it? Is aught amiss?" he asked.

"I have seen this portrait. It is one of myself, is it not?" Lucy asked coldly.

"To be sure, but when did you see it? I have been careful to cover it so that none should see it, not even Rebecca when she sat for me," Piers said, letting the canvas drop again. His gaze was direct and questioning, and the warmth had gone. Perhaps he suspected her of coming in here and prying! Lucy rose to defend herself.

"It was the day I returned from South-wark, after finding my foster-mother dead." She saw his eyes narrow; perhaps he had not known of Molly's death. Nevertheless, she would not spare him what she had come to say that night, to challenge him about the letter. Until that wretched portrait had robbed her of the power of speech.

"You may remember," she went on, "you told me I was a cause of disturbance here and suggested I should leave. I came here that night to talk to you, and overheard you talking to Rebecca outside. I'm sorry, I did not mean to eavesdrop, but I realised you were talking of your private plans. I knew I should not have heard such intimate conversation, so I hid behind the curtain. You yourself uncovered the portrait."

"So I remember," Piers murmured, "to allow it to dry. It was then you saw it?"

"By the moonlight from the window." Lucy's anger had congealed into frostiness now. "I found it a particularly offensive picture, and have no wish to see it again," she said in an unintentionally staccato voice. "Is that how you see me? Do you still believe me to be a wanton?"

Piers did not reply at once. He walked over to the window and looked out, thoughtfully. Lucy watched the dust specks floating in the sunlight over his black head, and wondered how long it would be before he spoke. Her anger was completely dissipated now. She only wished to get out of

227

this room, away from the portrait and this man she found so irresistibly attractive.

At long last he turned and regarded her.

"Lucy, I am sorry, truly sorry, about your foster-mother. It must have been a terrible blow for you. But I think you have been over-hasty in jumping to unwarrantable conclusions, as is your wont, little hot-head."

He smiled, and Lucy felt the familiar on-rush again.

"Hasty? In what way, may I ask?" she snapped.

"The moonlight can play deceptive tricks you know," he said gravely. "You saw in the portrait what you believed I saw in you. Let me show it to you again now, by daylight."

"No, no," she cried. "Are you determined always to ridicule me?" She bit her lip to try to bite back the anger, but it had to come out. " And it is not only the portrait – did you not relinquish me to Count Reichen-dorf in the belief that I was his whore? And laugh with Toby till you were near sick with laughing at the idea of defending my honour?" Lucy's eyes were flashing brittle lights of disdain at Piers now.

"I thank you, sir, for your offer of a birth-day gift," she said with a mocking low curtsey, holding her stiff gown wide, "and for my birthday outing. But," she continued rising to her full height and looking proudly up into his face, "I would be obliged if you would not make fun of me so long as I remain here. I too have my pride."

"Indeed, my fine lady, too much so," Piers said, laughing softly. "But some day when your temper is cooler, pray come and look at the portrait again by daylight, and you shall see I do not mock you. I am too fond of you, Lucy, to do so."

Lucy turned to go, flicking her skirts round furiously.

"Still you mock me – you, who are already betrothed! I have no love for Rebecca, but I can feel only pity for a woman about to marry a man who is so deceitful!"

It was Piers' turn to look cold and angry.

"What do you mean by that, Lucy?"

"I know you are to marry Rebecca, yet you try to make me fond of you!" Lucy cried. "And more than that – I saw you in Paris, burning the letter from the King! Added to everything else, you are a traitor – deny that if you dare!"

CHAPTER 18

Lucy was only too conscious of Piers' touch, burning and conjuring up a strangely violent emotion inside her as he tried to take her by the arm, but she shook him off furiously and fled from the room, fury closing her ears to his words.

"Lucy, Lucy!" he called after her, following her out in the corridor.

"I do not wish to hear you!" Lucy cried, nearly knocking Jennet off her feet as she swept around the corner and out of his sight.

Lucy felt too agitated to face anyone at this moment, least of all Elizabeth who would notice her distress and enquire the reason. And Mrs. Platt would hear a garbled account from Jennet of what she had witnessed upstairs, and all the kitchen staff would be agog to hear Lucy's explanation. Rather than face anyone, Lucy flung out of the door and down the steps and away, her mind reeling in confusion.

The sun's heat burst on her in all its strength as she emerged from the cool dimness of the house, and as she hurried along the street its fierce rays, reflected from the pavements, burned through the thin soles of her shoes. Without conscious thought, Lucy found herself walking by the river bank, and there she slowed her steps. Her agitation began to lessen.

There was a shimmering heat haze over the river. She watched the waters smooth-running as the tide ebbed, and thought sadly how the surface mirrored her own life – apparently smooth and carefree, but with complex undercurrents below governing the path of the waters. Down as far as the bridge the river ran swift and free, but then in its struggle to pass under the many small arches the waters swirled and eddied, fraught with their own power. Wherrymen seldom attempted to shoot the arches with their frail boats; one false move would mean instant destruction, caught up in the river's cruel vortex.

Lucy felt that at this moment she too was caught up in the same swift-running, pre-destined course as the river. There was no doubt in her mind now that she loved Piers, whatever he might be; but she resented the fact that he had encouraged her to become fond of him, knowing full well he was to be married. Lady Catherine had mistakenly thought that he cared for her too, but that was impossible. He would not ridicule her so, nor be marrying someone else, whatever the reason, if he loved her. He had too much strength of mind to do what he did not wish to do.

Oh, to be free to escape! But whither! Molly was dead and Lucy's love and loyalty for Elizabeth kept her chained to Kempston House, at least for the next few months.

Lucy sighed deeply, and turned to retrace her steps slowly towards Kempston House. However painful it might be, she was obliged to stay under the same roof as Piers. In a month Thomas would be taking Elizabeth to Longacre to await the birth of their child. Lucy would go with them, but Piers would probably remain in London, and as he had suggested that Rebecca should fix the wedding date for October or November, then in all probability Lucy and he would not meet again.

So there was only another month of Piers' proximity to bear; Lucy tried to console herself with this thought, but somehow it did not have the desired effect. Her temper completely vanished, and feeling utterly dispirited, Lucy turned into the courtyard of Kempston House.

Clattering carriage wheels behind made her turn quickly. Carew drove the coach and four into the yard and reined in the horses, then leapt down to open the carriage door. Rebecca alighted, her face shining with heat and pleasure, and clutching a swatch of material samples in one hand.

"Faugh! This heat!" She murmured, fanning herself vigorously and seeing Lucy's gaze on the samples she held, she held them forward as they entered the house.

"Aren't they magnificent?" she said, evidently highly satisfied. "I have just come from the dressmaker." She eyed Lucy a moment and then apparently decided to tell her some, if not all, of her news. "I am ordering a completely new wardrobe – these are the materials of the gowns I am to have. Just look at this glorious cinnamon velvet – and this crimson satin – and can you imagine this emerald silk trimmed with silver lace?"

She was glowing with excitement and happiness, but Lucy could only nod and agree dully that they were indeed magnificent and should become Rebecca well. How could she tell her she knew this was Rebecca's wedding trousseau?

In the vestibule Rebecca abandoned her to rush off and show Elizabeth her samples, while Lucy went below to the kitchen, wondering what Mrs. Platt would think of her long absence.

Mrs. Platt, however, did not seem to notice aught amiss. She was bustling about her cauldrons and chafing dishes, for the family would soon expect dinner to be served.

"Come on, Jennet lass," she was saying, "the salt box I said, not the spice box. Oh Lucy, I'm glad you're here." She rolled her eyes heavenwards. Lucy looked at Jennet, standing holding the spice box, eyes wide and uncomprehending, her mouth sagging slackly.

"I don't know," Mrs. Platt said across her head to Lucy, "she was slow and clumsy enough before, but since she lost her family last year of the plague, she seems to have lost what few wits she had. "Shaking her head, she forgot Jennet's problem to return to her own more immediate ones. Jennet melted into the corner of the grate, next to the spit, and crouched there, mumbling to herself.

Poor child, Lucy thought as she fetched dishes and plates, no wonder Rebecca finds her irritating and beats her, but that in turn only makes her worse. Perhaps the child would have a welcome respite from beatings when Rebecca left for Longacre with Thomas the following week.

As luck would have it, Jennet was to come in for one more thrashing before the week was out. She came running and shrieking into the kitchen one hot, sultry morning.

"Whatever is it now?" Mrs. Platt looked up from her pestle and mortar.

"I only spilt water!" the girl shrieked, her arms pressed tightly across her head. She sank on the flagstoned floor at Lucy's feet, moaning, as Rebecca stormed in.

"You stupid, clumsy idiot!" Rebecca raved. "My best bedgown and my coverlet are absolutely soaked!" She pulled Jennet up by the arm and rained blows on her head, her face scarlet with fury. "Why can't you learn, you misbegotten cretin!" She thumped and pounded the child's head and shoulders until eventually her arm tired and her anger dimmed.

"By're lady," she panted. "I swear, the very

next time you perform any clumsy action, my girl, I shall kill you – you hear me? I'll kill you!" she hissed in Jennet's face, and grabbing her by the ear she dragged the whimpering child roughly down the cellar steps.

Lucy heard the sound of the bolt on the coalhole door shooting home. Rebecca re-emerged from the cellar, still red-faced but calmer now.

"She is to be left there until this evening, is that clear? I shall not risk her doing any more damage today," she said briskly, then turned to Lucy. "See what you can do about my bedgown and coverlet, will you, Lucy? I have no desire to sleep between damp sheets tonight."

She swept out. Mrs. Platt shrugged her shoulders and returned to her grinding without comment, so Lucy went up to Rebecca's chamber. It was stiflingly close and hot in there. She threw open the casement and draped the coverlet over the sill, and the gown over a chair. In this sultry heat they would be dry before midday.

As she walked along the corridor she heard voices from Elizabeth's chamber.

"They are simply beautiful, Rebecca," she heard Elizabeth's light voice say. "Which gown will you choose for the wedding feast?"

"I know not yet," was Rebecca's careless reply. "That depends on what colour my bridegroom wears. I know he has ordered a black silk camelot suit with gold lace sleeve bands, and a peacock blue ferrandin with silver lace. Can you imagine how we should clash if he wore the blue and I the emerald green?"

Lucy heard the sound of laughter, then Elizabeth continued.

"Ah, but the blue will suit his dark curly hair and dark eyes well."

Lucy hurried away, trying to banish the vision of Piers in his wedding finery, holding Rebecca's hand and gazing at her with love in his eyes. It was too cruel, to watch the man she loved marrying a woman she disliked intensely. Please God she could avoid the wedding!

In the afternoon Lucy unlocked Jennet from the coalhole. Rebecca would have forgotten the incident by now, and would probably forget to order her release too. Jennet emerged, grimy face streaked with tear tracks but dry-eyed now and silent. There was a sunken look about her eyes as she cowered sullenly in the chimney corner.

For the remainder of that last week before Rebecca and Thomas left Jennet remained thus, neither speaking nor answering anyone who spoke to her, and only jerking suddenly to life when she heard Rebecca's call. Then she would scamper off with fear-filled eyes, as fast as her legs would carry her.

When Saturday morning came and the household had waved off Thomas and Rebecca and an excited Mother Benson, Lucy expected to see Jennet sigh with relief, but Rebecca's departure did not seem to register on her dulled brain. She started guiltily, the whites of her eyes prominent when Lucy spoke to her.

"Easy now, Jennet," Lucy said kindly, "no-one will harm you, and there will be no more beatings for a week or so." The girl stared at her blankly. Lucy sighed, and went to tidy the chaos Rebecca had left in her wake after packing.

Elizabeth was feeling the effect of the heat more than usual. As Lucy handed her her posset before bed she patted her protuberant stomach and said, "I' faith, I shall not be sorry to put down this burden, Lucy, if this sultry weather is to continue much longer."

" 'T will not be long," Lucy replied. "What

is it now – four or five weeks? 'T will soon pass."

Elizabeth sighed as Lucy tucked her up comfortably for the night and doused the candles.

"Sleep well, Elizabeth," Lucy said at the door.

"I will – if this restive mare of a child is of a mood to sleep too," Elizabeth laughed sleepily.

Lucy closed the door and went to her own chamber. She wondered what Piers was doing for she had not seen him since he waved Thomas and Rebecca off from the doorstep. Presently she heard his footsteps pass by her door. He was humming "Belle qui tient ma vie."

CHAPTER 19

Lucy stirred and awoke from a troubled sleep. She lay still, wondering what had disturbed her. Was that a faint smell of burning she could detect? Had Jennet forgotten to damp down the kitchen fire?

She arose quickly, drawing a wrap about her shoulders. Out in the corridor there was no trace of the faintly acrid odour at all, and she returned to her room. Yes, surely it was still there?

There was no hearth in Lucy's room, and the candles had all been carefully doused. She crossed to the window and looked out. Away across the rooftops to the east there was a flush of pink low in the night sky. When Lucy pushed the lattice window open, the pungent smell was borne in heavily on the warm September air.

It was far away, and house fires were a regular occurrence, Lucy well knew. Wooden lath and plaster houses were ready fuel in hot, dry weather such as this, but parish overseers had seen to the provision of fire buckets and pumps in most areas so that they were soon extinguished. There was no cause for alarm.

She re-crossed the room, intending to go back to bed, but the sound of soft foot-steps out in the corridor arrested her. Elizabeth – she must go and reassure her. Lucy opened the door and ran out. Piers, still in shirt and breeches, was standing at the window at the end of the corridor. Hearing her, he turned and raised a finger to his lips.

"Ssssh! There is no cause for alarm," he said in a whisper. "You smelt it too?"

Lucy nodded. "It is far away to the east, and the wind has been a westerly one all the week," he went on. He paused outside Elizabeth's door and listened. "Elizabeth is breathing deeply so I think she is still sound asleep. No need to disturb her. Go back to bed, Lucy, all is well."

Lucy was conscious of his eyes on her back, burning her as she went back to her chamber. She slept little for the rest of that night, tossing and turning restlessly till the sheets became clammy with the heat and she tossed them aside. That reminded her of the fever, when Piers' face had appeared before her from time to time and she had spat out her hatred of men and of him in particular. And of how Elizabeth had told her Piers had nursed her. Did he still remember the terrible things she had said in her delirium? How could she explain to him that her hatred of men was born out of the cruel treatment she had seen Molly bear at the hands of selfish men?

Until she came to Kempston House Lucy had believed all men to be grasping and greedy, satisfying their desires and then casting aside a creature they no longer had any use for. Now she knew otherwise. No man could have been kinder and more considerate than both Thomas and Piers had been. She began to regret her hasty judgement. Perhaps some day she could explain to Piers. She would like to have his good opinion of her, if nothing else.

Soon dawn broke. Lucy hurried to Elizabeth's chamber and found her already up and dressed.

"There was a smell of burning," Elizabeth explained, "but it is nothing, I think. The glow has disappeared from the sky."

Lucy and Elizabeth ate breakfast together, Piers not yet having appeared. Soon after they had finished eating he hurried in,

242

dressed in outdoor clothes. Elizabeth looked at him in surprise.

"Have you been out riding so early?" she asked.

"Yes, I went to discover the origin of the fire," he replied. " 'T was the King's baker relighting his ovens after the Sabbath, they say, and somehow the fire got out of hand and set fire to other houses in the street."

"Has it been extinguished now?" Lucy asked him.

"No – not yet. I shall go back there shortly to see if Carew and I can help. There is no need to concern yourself, however. May I have a word with you, Lucy?"

He was waiting for her in the vestibule. Lucy looked up at him expectantly. His expression was sombre.

"The fire had spread further than I thought, Lucy. From the bakehouse sparks blew across to an inn yard opposite and set light to the hay, then to the warehouses in Thames Street. From Pudding Lane, where it began, it has spread the length of Fish street as far as London Bridge. At least three hundred houses have been gutted already, and people are beginning to panic and run."

His expression softened when he saw Lucy's dismay. "There is no danger here, though, provided the people keep their wits and fight it. We are well out of harm's way. I must take Carew and go back to help. Do you keep Elizabeth happy and reassured, and I shall return ere long."

He swung around and hastened away without further ado. Lucy returned slowly to Elizabeth, who was standing at the window, looking out.

"There is a heavy pall of smoke over there," she commented quietly. " 'Tis a larger fire than we are accustomed to. Do you think they will be able to quell it when the warehouses are full of wood and oil and rosin?"

"To be sure," Lucy said soothingly. "There are buckets ready in all the churches, and longhandled firehooks to pull down blazing timber, not to mention the new fire engines; they can pump water at a fine old rate!"

Elizabeth seemed content enough with her reply, Lucy was relieved to see, for she turned her attention now to choosing the fare for dinner. Some time later, Lucy went down to the kitchen.

Mrs. Platt was up to her elbows in soapsuds. "Got to do it myself," she said drily, "the laundress and the cleaning woman ran off when Carew told them of the fire. Seems

244

they had a look from up on the leads and thought their own homes might be in danger. Now Carew's gone with Master Piers, there's only me and Jennet left."

She jerked her head to indicate the inert Jennet, lolling stupidly in the chimney corner. Lucy could see her problem ... Jennet was useless.

"Never mind, I shall do the cooking, Mrs. Platt; mayhap Lady Elizabeth would like to help too." Smiling at the horrified look on Mrs. Platt's face, Lucy went back to Elizabeth.

Later that evening she was shocked to see Piers in the vestibule, blackened with grime, wiping the soot from his face with the back of his hand.

"The wind has freshened and changed to easterly," he told her curtly. "Added to that, the people are terrified out of their wits and are making no attempt to fight the fire, but are grabbing their valuables and fleeing. The river is choked with boats, all of them piled high with household goods and their owners fighting and screaming in panic. At this rate the fire may well threaten us here, far removed as we are."

"Are we to pack and go?" Lucy asked him. She felt fear rising inside her, but Elizabeth must be protected and kept calm.

"No," he answered quietly. "Not yet. I hear the Duke of York and the King are on their way. Out of the love they bear for His Majesty, the people may stand and fight yet.

"I shall send Carew to Toby's house, to warn him that you and Elizabeth and the servants may be obliged to seek shelter there if need be. In the meantime, do you secrete whatever valuables you can in the cellars."

"Am I to speak of this to Elizabeth?" Lucy asked.

He considered a moment. "Tell her we are storing the silver plate and Thomas's papers and books down in the cellars for safety, but stress that the possibility of fire here is remote. Then she may add her jewellery and whatever else she values.

"Lock the cellars tightly. They are all of stone, and the kitchen floor is stone flag-ged." He turned to go again, but paused at the door. "You had better store Rebecca's wedding gown for safety also," he added, and disappeared out of the door.

Even in emergency he had consideration for others, Lucy reflected. That being so, she would put down in the cellars the portraits he cared so much about, although he had not mentioned them, the ones of Rebecca and Thomas in the gallery first, then the new one of Rebecca, probably destined to be the gift to the bride from the bridegroom she thought sadly. And even, she resolved, since he had said he treasured it, the one she hated of herself.

Casually she told Elizabeth of Piers' suggestion to put her jewellery in a safe place, hoping Elizabeth would not be alarmed.

"An excellent idea," Elizabeth agreed quickly, and set about collecting her valuables together. In the meantime Lucy removed the portraits from the gallery then went to Piers' studio.

It was still daylight, and though the sun still shone, its rays could not penetrate the heavy layer of smoke that enveloped the city. Lucy saw Rebecca's portrait standing against the wall, and the other one on the easel still covered. She went to gather up one under each arm, but stopped. She felt a twinge of curiosity to see her own picture once more. Did it still look as unkind, as wanton, as she remembered it?

She flung back the hessian covering and stood back. The vivid colours of the emerald green gown and flaming red hair almost took her breath away. But as she gazed she realised this was no cruel portrayal but a candid reflection of the girl she had been when Piers knew her. The tilt of the head was proud rather than defiant, and the expression of the mouth and eyes was not hard and mocking as she had thought, but rather independent and full of fire.

Lucy felt the soothing effect of anger softening into understanding. The brash colours of the portrait were subtly linked by fine nuances of shading and expression that softened the whole effect. By moonlight she had seen only garish blatancy, and missed the subtlety and affection. Yes, there was undoubtedly affection in every line of it. Lucy felt a warmth, a glowing happiness, course through her veins. Even if she did not have Piers' love, she had his affection and respect. With care she carried the portraits down to the cellar.

Evening tried to darken into night, but the angry red glow refused to let the darkness come. Piers came home, filthy and dishevelled and fiercely hungry. Elizabeth, reassured once more, went to bed while Lucy sat and talked to Piers as he ate, telling him which valuables she had disposed of in the cellar.

"Good," he commented briefly. "The threat of fire is still far removed, but it is as well to be prepared."

"It is under control then?" Lucy asked.

"Not yet. I shall sleep and then return to help again in the morning," Piers replied. Lucy could see his eyes were red-rimmed from the smoke and need of sleep.

Next morning he was gone again with Carew before dawn. Elizabeth surveyed the scene from the window.

"Heavens, Lucy! Half of the city is ablaze!" she cried, "and there are people running backwards and forwards down there, I can see them through the smoke!"

"They are those whose homes have been destroyed. Piers say they are setting up camps outside the city walls," Lucy explained. She could not tell Elizabeth all Piers had told her – how some of the people had gone berserk with the sounds of destruction ringing in their ears, how they had pushed each other heedlessly in their panic to escape, or looted and robbed mercilessly. Nor did she tell Elizabeth that while she slept there had been no night; the sky aflame had remained as bright as the day had been.

Despite its distance the sound of destruction thundered ominously like a storm. Perhaps, Lucy thought, she had better warn

Elizabeth to expect to hear sudden explosions. Piers had said the King was to order houses to be blown up in an attempt to starve the fire of yet more tinder-dry fuel.

Jennet came into the room to clear the table.

"Jennet, will you tell Mrs. Platt I shall come down shortly to prepare the dinner?" Elizabeth said to her. Jennet continued stacking the dishes, oblivious to her words. "Jennet – Jennet, listen to me," Elizabeth said.

Jennet looked up. Seeing Elizabeth's face she made a determined effort to try to understand her mistress.

"Tell–Mrs.–Platt–I–shall–prepare–dinner–soon," Elizabeth repeated slowly and clearly. Jennet gazed and concentrated a moment, then smiled and nodded. Elizabeth turned to Lucy.

"I hope Piers is taking care of himself down there. I have never seen such a fire in my life."

Lucy heard Jennet muttering as she carried the tray from the table.

"Fire down there, fire down there," she murmured, then suddenly she came to a halt and turned. "Fire?" she repeated, and her nostrils twitched. Catching the scent of woodsmoke, she dropped the tray with a deafening clatter to the floor. "Fire!" she screamed. "Fire!" and the whites of her eyes glistened in terror.

"Don't take on so, child," soothed Elizabeth, hurrying towards her, arms outstretched. But she did not see the little silver salt dish that had rolled silently from the tray across the floor to her feet. Lucy watched, horror-struck, as she saw Elizabeth stumble, clutch at the air for support, then fall, overbalanced by her own cumbersome weight.

Lucy leapt up in alarm and ran to help Elizabeth rise.

"Elizabeth! Are you all right?" she cried, sliding her arm under her back and raising her head.

Elizabeth nodded. "All is well," she said, rather dazed. "Help me to a chair, Lucy." Lucy supported her to the chair, and settled her there. Then she turned on Jennet.

"You clumsy child!" she cried, more out of relieved fright than anger. "You could have done some terrible mischief!"

Jennet had been standing open-mouthed since her scream, dumbstruck at the repercussions. Realisation slowly dawned in the poor muddled brain that she had been responsible for Elizabeth's fall, and slowly her eyes widened in terror of the consequences. Automatically she threw her arms across her head to protect herself from the inevitable blow when Lucy cried out, and she cowered, whining, against the wall.

"Leave her, Lucy," said Elizabeth weakly. "She is not accountable for her actions, poor child." She turned her head and spoke softly to the girl. "Hush, child, there is no need to fear. No one shall harm you."

But Jennet was not listening. Her eyes were rolling piteously, and Lucy could guess she was remembering Rebecca's last threat – "The very next time you are clumsy, my girl, I shall kill you!" she had hissed venomously, and Jennet knew Rebecca usually carried out her threats.

"Fire – kill you!" Jennet whined, then louder, "Fire, kill!" she cried, and casting an anguished look of fear all around her, she ran from the room, howling.

Lucy walked quickly towards the door after her.

"Let her go," said Elizabeth quietly. Lucy looked back and saw Elizabeth was lying back in the chair, eyes closed, and a sickly pallor was creeping over her taut face.

Lucy hurried to her side. "Elizabeth? Do

you not feel well?" she asked, full of concern lest the fall should have occasioned some damage to her.

"I think the fall has shaken me a little," Elizabeth admitted faintly. "I think it were best I lay down a while. Will you help me to bed?"

Anxiously Lucy helped her return to her chamber. That clumsy child, Jennet! Perhaps it would be wise to send for the family's physician, to ensure no harm had been done.

Lucy went down to the kitchen. There was no sign of either Jennet or of Mrs. Platt, and the kitchen was full of smoke. She went out into the kitchen garden and could see the fire was closer now on that side of the house, possibly less than a mile away.

She sought throughout the house and garden but it became evident that both Jennet and Mrs. Platt had gone. Jennet's fright had no doubt driven her away, but had Mrs. Platt also panicked at the nearness of the fire and run away without warning?

No matter, Lucy thought. Piers and Carew should be back soon. If the fire approached too near, she could remove Elizabeth to safety herself.

Lucy climbed the stairs again to Elizabeth's chamber. She must ask her to be ready to depart at a moment's notice, if the need arose.

But she stopped short in the doorway. Elizabeth's white face stared at her unbelievingly from across the room. She was gripping the back of a chair, her back arched in pain.

"Lucy?" she said pathetically. "Oh Lucy! I'm so sorry, but I think it has begun! I think the babe is to be born today!"

CHAPTER 20

Lucy gaped at Elizabeth in horror. There was no one else in the house to help, not even Jennet, and Mother Benson, who was the only person who knew aught of delivering infants, was gone to Longacre!

She hastened to Elizabeth. "Are you in great pain?" she asked her, putting an arm about her and guiding her towards the bed.

"Only now and again, there is an ache low in my back. There it is again!" Elizabeth's face tightened as a contraction gripped her. Momentarily Lucy felt panic-stricken. What did she know of delivering a babe, apart from hearsay and the vivid accounts Molly had rendered of her own ordeals, aided by the local gossip?

Resolutely, Lucy forced the panic out of her mind. She *must* help Elizabeth; there was no one else. With luck, Piers would return soon, and by all accounts a woman's labour lasted several hours if not days, so there was time yet to send him for a physician. She could cope. She only prayed that the fire kept its distance from the house, for now Elizabeth was no longer in a state to be moved.

Elizabeth lay on the bed, white as a ghost. Now and again she moaned softly and rolled from side to side, then as the pain passed she lay still and pale as a dead creature again. She looked even more fragile and ethereal than ever, Lucy thought, despite her grossness, and her vulnerability wrenched at Lucy's heart.

Beads of perspiration began to form on Elizabeth's upturned face and roll slowly down, darkening her fair hair. Tenderly Lucy bathed her, cursing the heat of the September day and of the fire that was making Elizabeth's struggle worse.

"It's so hot and airless in here, Lucy," Elizabeth said piteously between bouts of pain. "Open the window, I beg you."

As Lucy did so the stench of the smoke and roaring noise of the fire entered the chamber yet more strongly. And at the same time there came the clatter of hooves in the courtyard below.

Moments later Piers knocked and strode into the chamber.

"God grant we shall never see the like again!" he exclaimed to Lucy. "The very lead melts from the rooftops and flows down the streets in a stream! The Lord Mayor is weeping in the streets like a child because none will heed him and try to quench the fire. There is little hope, Lucy, it will cover the whole city before 'tis done. It would be best we took Elizabeth to Toby's house now, before it comes too close."

He turned then, his eyes scouring the room for Elizabeth. It was little wonder he had not seen her, Lucy thought; she lay silent and for the moment inert on the bed, and in her pallor there was little to choose in colour between her and the sheets.

Lucy heard Piers catch his breath. "Elizabeth! Are you ill?" he cried. He strode quickly to her side and took her hand.

Elizabeth groaned and stirred. Lucy looked up at Piers and said softly, "You cannot move her now, Piers, she is in labour with the child."

Piers looked bewildered. "But 't was not to be yet – a month, Thomas said..." He knelt at Elizabeth's side.

"She fell ... an accident; it has caused the babe to move, I think," Lucy explained.

"Fell?" There was anger in his voice, but

Elizabeth groaned again and he did not demand an explanation. "What can we do for her?" he looked up at Lucy expectantly.

"Go fetch the physician, Piers; there is naught else you can do here. The fire does not threaten us yet, and it will take some time yet before the child is born. I can manage till then. But get a doctor here to deliver the child."

Piers wasted no further time talking. Moments later Lucy heard the sound of his horse galloping out of the gateway and mingle with the distant roar of the fire.

Elizabeth sighed deeply. "The pains come more closely all the time, Lucy."

"Is it bad, Elizabeth? Shall I give you wine?"

"Thank you, no. Oh, the heat!" Elizabeth drew a hand across her brow again. "What o'clock is it?"

Lucy realised that despite the heat and the brightness outside, it was in fact approaching evening. The city appeared a solid sheet of flame for miles on end. There would be no night again tonight.

A sudden thought caused Lucy's heart to flutter. In her anxiety over Elizabeth she had forgotten that others at this time would be in need of physicians. No doubt every doctor in London was involved in tending those who must have been wounded. Buildings were crashing in great flaming ruins, and not everyone could have escaped unharmed.

She hoped Piers would find someone, if not their own physician, in time to cope with the birth.

She sat on the bed by Elizabeth, bathing her head and soothing her, and giving her sips of water and then just sat holding her hand. Gradually Elizabeth slipped into a quiet sleep.

Lucy paced anxiously to the window. Above the fiery glow she could catch intermittent glimpses of St. Paul's as the smoke revealed it now and again, silhouetted starkly against the crimson skyline.

She remember how Elizabeth always used to pray for help to God, and although Lucy had never been accustomed to praying, she did so now.

"Please God, help Elizabeth and Piers. The two I love most in the world are in danger – protect them both, I pray. Let me not fail them as I failed Molly. God help us, please!"

As she stood there, clenching her hands and praying, she saw the dark shape of St.

Paul's suddenly begin to glow, then slowly flames began to envelope it. For a time it stood glowing like a gigantic candle, then hung for a critical moment before crumbling and crashing to the ground.

Suddenly there was a further rumbling roar and on another part of the skyline mountainous sparks leapt and danced like fireworks. Elizabeth started awake and sat up.

"Oh God! Oh Lucy!" she cried.

"Have no fear, Elizabeth, it is but the houses they are blowing up to halt the fire," Lucy hastened to assure her, but Elizabeth was not listening. She gripped Lucy's hands, her eyes staring.

"It's coming!" she cried, and a look of exultation replaced the look of terror. Her nails dug into Lucy's palms and she gripped fiercely and strained, teeth clenched and the muscles of her face rigid. Lucy willed the panic out of her mind; now, for Elizabeth, she must be calm.

The moment passed. Elizabeth lay, limp and exhausted and panting quickly. Her eyes were shining; she was unaware of all danger, conscious only that now her pain was to some end, soon her child would be born.

In a moment of respite Lucy hurried round the chamber, preparing a sheet to receive the child, pouring more water into a bowl. A knife! There was a cord to be cut, she remembered Molly saying. Oh God! help me to do the right thing!

She found the knife, and squatted by Elizabeth again. After the next struggle she found herself praying once more, praying for Piers' safety, down there in that holocaust. Dear God send him back! Even to Rebecca's arms, so long as he was safe!

Elizabeth began to strain and heave again, sweat standing out in glistening droplets on her face and arms. Then suddenly, with a long-drawn sigh, she lay back. To her amazement, Lucy saw the baby's head, and as Elizabeth gave a final push, the tiny body glided into her waiting hands. She stared at it, speechless.

It was over – so soon – the child was born! Gathering her wits, she cut the cord that still bound it to its mother. Seeing the blood ooze from the severed end, it seemed only common sense to tie it off, to prevent the child bleeding to death. Twine from Elizabeth's desk solved the problem, and as she tied the knot, a thin wail rose from the creature.

Elizabeth was watching her, wide-eyed. "My babe – he is alive and well?"

Lucy nodded and smiled. "You are right – you have a son, Elizabeth. Thomas will be so proud of you."

She laid the child aside on the sheet, and tended Elizabeth. Thank you, God, Lucy said inwardly, but watch over us yet. Elizabeth's eyes were closing contentedly and the babe fast asleep when Lucy went to lean on the windowsill.

She heard a clatter on the cobblestones below. Piers? Her heart leapt, but the wheels of a cart clattered on past the house. Eddies of thick smoke were wheeling about the house now. How close had the fire crept up while she had been preoccupied with Elizabeth? Lucy ran downstairs to investigate.

Thick streamers of smoke were wreathing upwards from under the door of Thomas's study. Lucy flung the door open. The room was invisible, smoke gushing out into the corridor all around Lucy, followed, to her horror, by little tongues of flame. She pulled the door hastily shut again.

Heaven preserve us! the thought raced through her brain, the house is afire! There was no time to be lost in getting Elizabeth and the babe to safety!

She raced up the stairs, tripping and cursing her damnable, inconvenient skirts. She rolled the child tightly in his sheet and put him on the end of the bed while she roused Elizabeth.

"Come quickly," she said softly but urgently. "Elizabeth, come, wake up!"

Elizabeth murmured drowsily, but obeyed, letting Lucy slip a blanket around her shoulders.

Thank God she is too stunned to realise what is happening, Lucy thought, and she dragged Elizabeth to her feet, pulling one sleepy arm over her own shoulders. Then she tried to catch up the baby under her arm, but it was impossible to do so without Elizabeth sliding gently floorwards.

I'll have to leave him, she thought. Get Elizabeth out to safety first, then there should still be time to run back for him. But move fast, for pity's sake, Elizabeth!

She dragged a tottering, reluctant Elizabeth towards the door, and propped her against the wall while she opened it. Then she continued their unsteady, lurching progress along the corridor to the stairs.

Dense smoke was swirling up the staircase towards them. Lucy leaned the weight of Elizabeth's body against the balustrade, then pulled her blanket to cover both their faces. Then she let Elizabeth's weight begin to slide down the banister, putting her own body in front to check her.

Struggling and stumbling, fighting for breath and half-choked, Lucy finally got Elizabeth down into the hall. Thank God, the heavy door of Thomas's study was still closed, but blackened and charred, and it could not be long before the flames burst through.

Elizabeth was coughing now, and this seemed to bring her to her senses. By the time Lucy reached the rear door leading to the garden, Elizabeth was able to co-operate, though weakly.

Outside they both gasped lungsful of fresh air, then Elizabeth cried, "My child – where is he?"

"I'll get him, fear not," said Lucy. "Come, to the gazebo, quickly." Elizabeth tried to turn back, but Lucy coaxed her on. "You'll be safe there, beyond the pool the fire will not reach you, and there is still time for me to fetch the babe. But quickly!"

Elizabeth was in no state to argue. She turned her large, trustful eyes to Lucy and nodded, then stumbled on with Lucy's support.

In the little summerhouse Lucy lowered Elizabeth on to the bench seat and threw the blanket over her, "I shall be back instantly," she called as she turned and ran back towards the house.

The fire would not be able to reach Elizabeth there – long lawns and the little bridge over the lily pool and stone-flagged paths lay between the house and the gazebo, and the fire would find readier fuel in other directions.

Lucy glanced towards the city as she neared the house. The sky, like molten copper, was throbbing with green and purple flashes of light, till her eyes ached from looking. She darted into the choking fog, holding her breath as she ran to the stairs. Flames had now reached from the study to the vestibule and were licking hungrily at the foot of the banisters. Lucy hesitated a fraction of a second, then picking up her skirts, held them tightly round her waist and plunged through.

At the head of the stairs, coughing and choking and with tears blinding her eyes, Lucy had to feel her way along the wall, for nothing was to be seen through the smoke. She heard a high-pitched sound above the roar and crackle of the flames – the babe was crying! Guided by the thin wail, she found her way to the still open door of Elizabeth's chamber.

Groping her way to the bed, she snatched up the wriggling bundle, and its cries ceased. The sheet was wet; so much the better, she thought, pulling the damp mass over the baby's face.

She pulled her own woollen skirt up over her shoulders and head, like a fishwife's shawl, and wrapped the baby tightly inside against her chest, and blundered out along the corridor again. Progress was completely blind now, for she could not even extricate her arms from her skirt to feel her way.

A glow met her at the staircase. Flames leapt dully through the smoke from the hall below. The heat was overpowering, and Lucy felt faint. There was no exit that way!

The servant's staircase! Back she blundered, slipping and stumbling, almost overcome by the smoke and heat. She could feel tiny explosive coughs from the baby against her chest – she *must* get out, must save Elizabeth's baby! Oh Piers! Where are you?

The stone staircase was smoke-clogged but as yet no fire had reached there. Gratefully Lucy ran down, but as she turned to descend the second flight, a solid sheet of flame faced her at the bottom, its fierce heat frizzling the hair that stood out from her shawl.

Dear God, was there no escape? Lucy stood rooted in utter panic, and at that moment a deafening crash met her ears. The solid beams of the house were giving way. In seconds more she would be trapped under their weight! But what could she do? To plunge into the wall of flame before her was unthinkable!

Lucy felt tears of frustration and despair on her eyelids, drying as they welled. Dear God, do not desert me now, she prayed. I can do no more!

She felt her strength giving out. Her knees were buckling. She leaned on the wall and felt its heat burning through her shawl. Faintly she heard the baby begin to wail, then she sank slowly – unresistingly – to the floor...

CHAPTER 21

On the brink of unconsciousness Lucy was halted. Someone was calling her name. "Lucy! Lucy!" she heard dimly floating through the fog that enclosed her. As in a dream she saw a filthy face, determined and grimly unsmiling and framed in grizzled hair, looming before her. Lucy struggled to rise.

"I am here!" she gasped, and the face bent over her. Molly, come to save the babe from the fire, as she had done once before – dear Molly!

Lucy felt something warm and wet thrown over her, and someone lifting her bodily. Automatically her arms tightened around the child, and then she was thrown upside down over someone's shoulder. Then suddenly there was a rending, roaring crash and a fearful weight smote her hard across her back, and amidst a colossal shower of sparks and debris Lucy felt herself falling ... falling.

Much later, it seemed, Lucy awoke from the dream. All around her the brazen glow persisted, but at a distance. She was lying in the gazebo, and before her stood a pair of legs clad in filthy breeches. Looking up, she saw Piers' blackened face gazing anxiously down at her.

"Lucy, I thought I'd lost you," he murmured hoarsely, and knelt beside her. "When that beam hit us," he said as he folded her to him, and kissed her gently on the forehead, "I thought it had killed you. Oh Lucy!"

Lucy thought she must still be dreaming. No matter, she thought blissfully, 't was a wonderful dream, let it go on. A baby began to howl. The child – Elizabeth – the fire! The memory came rushing back. The staircase – her collapse – Molly, no, not Molly, Piers!

She pushed Piers away and looked up at him. He was real enough, she could feel the hard muscles of his arms beneath her finger-tips. She could have laughed aloud – at herself for mistaking Piers for Molly, and for sheer joy and relief.

Suddenly she felt anxious.

"Where is Elizabeth?" she asked urgently.

"Toby has taken her to Silsbury House,

and we shall follow when you feel well enough to ride." Piers turned as the babe began to cry lustily again. He picked him up and laid a finger on the little wrinkled cheek.

"I' faith, his eyes are exactly the same as Elizabeth's," he murmured in surprise. "It is a boy, is it not?"

"Allow me to introduce you," said Lucy with a smile. "Master Piers, your nephew, as yet unnamed." Piers bowed his head in acknowledgement. Then Lucy remembered. "Piers – the physician, could you not find one? What kept you away so long? Did you not see Kempston House was in danger from the fire too?"

"Hold hard – one question at a time," Piers smiled, then became instantly serious again. "There were no doctors to be found in the whole of London. I spurred poor Bess on almost to death in that heat in my search. The people were crazed with fear; they believed the fire was a deliberate plot by the Dutch or the Papists, and attacked anyone who got in their way. I was near distracted, Lucy, when I came upon the King, in shirt and breeches and knee-deep in water, handing buckets along in a chain.

"He was kindness itself, despite the grave

situation. He bade me go to Whitehall and fetch Dr. Charlton, one of his own physicians-in-ordinary, to tend Elizabeth. But when I reached Whitehall the doctor had gone to St. James's to tend one of the Queen's ladies, and I had the devil's own job to reach him. However, he is with Elizabeth now at Toby's, so she is in good hands."

Lucy regarded him with new respect and understanding. Only then did she notice how his hair, once black, was shrivelled and grey from the flames, his face bruised and cut and his arms, showing through the torn sleeves, were a mass of raw flesh and blisters. Pity and annoyance with herself rushed to the fore.

"Piers – you are hurt!" she cried.

Piers smiled wanly. "Come," he said. "Bess should be sufficiently rested now to carry us to Toby's. And there's another young man here the physician should see," he added, indicating the babe. Lucy took the child from him and he led her out to where Bess stood tethered, the whites of her eyes showing her fear despite the distance from the roaring flames.

Piers swung Lucy up on the saddle and climbed up before her, then in moments they were cantering through the gardens of

Kempston House to the rear gate and away from the holocaust.

Growing more and more faint as they rode, Lucy dimly remembered arriving at Silsbury House and going to bed. For two days she slept exhausted, and knew nothing of the soothing unguents that were applied to her blistered limbs. The third day, stiff and sore, she was reunited with Elizabeth.

Now the whole episode seemed but a hideous nightmare. In that case, she wondered, had she dreamed Piers' kisses in the gazebo as she recovered consciousness?

Elizabeth lay, pale but serene and contented, in a vast canopied bed, the infant asleep in a cot alongside. His presence proved it had been no dream.

"Doctor Charlton has nothing but praise for you, for coping with the birthing so admirably, Lucy. He said he himself could have done no better," she said, taking Lucy's hand. "I cannot express my gratitude, Lucy, and I know Thomas will be overjoyed. Toby has sent word to him, and doubtless he will return to London post-haste. Oh Lucy!" she said with a start as Lucy bent her head, "your beautiful hair – it is all scorched and burned!"

" 'T is nothing, I shall cut it and it will

grow again as red and strong as ever," Lucy laughed. She remembered Piers' once-black hair, now grey and burned. "How is Piers, Elizabeth? Have you seen him?"

"Not yet, but Dr. Charlton has tended him and Carew says he is well, thank God. You know Carew worships Piers as a spaniel does its master. His eyes filled with tears as he spoke of Piers fighting through the flames to find a doctor, completely mindless of his own safety. He is a fine man, Lucy."

Lucy nodded. "I know. I hope Rebecca will appreciate his qualities," she said, trying to swallow the lump in her throat.

"Rebecca? Why Rebecca?" Elizabeth asked.

Lucy bit her lip. She was not supposed to know.

"I'm sorry. I overheard your private discussion, but truly, I was not eavesdropping, Elizabeth. I heard Piers and Rebecca talking of the marriage settlement, and later I heard you and Rebecca discussing the wedding clothes."

There was a pause, then Elizabeth's bell-like laugh rang out.

"Oh Lucy! You misunderstood! Thomas is settling a dowry on Rebecca so that she may marry Toby! Whatever made you think it was Piers? He and Rebecca get along well as cousins, but as husband and wife – oh, never!"

She seemed to find the idea highly amusing, and Lucy was glad of her merriment to conceal her own confusion. She felt ashamed of the pleasure she felt. Of course! What a fool she had been! When they had talked of the bridegroom's dark, curly hair, her impetuous, jealous mind had jumped to the wrong conclusion. What other evidence had she had – a cousinly kiss goodnight? That signified nothing, except to a mind clouded with jealousy. Lucy was ashamed and angry with herself.

As soon as she could, she left Elizabeth and wandered restlessly about Silsbury House. From a landing window she could see that the fire away to the north in London was evidently abating, but the sky above was a solid blanket of smoke cloud, miles in length. It was a strangely unfamiliar view of London with most of its graceful spires missing.

She wandered on through corridors and passages, until she found herself in an apparently disused part of the house. Flurries of dust rose about her as her skirts swished along the floor, and she could see her own footprints behind her. An oaken door faced her. Idly Lucy turned the knob and went in.

She found herself in a sombre chamber, well-furnished but shrouded in dust. Over the mantel hung a portrait of a young woman, a girl of about her own age, a lovely red-haired creature with a luminous glow about her pale face. Something about the portrait captured Lucy's attention, and she drew closer. On the frame she read the words "Lady Sarah, 1647".

Again she looked at the face – and caught her breath. No wonder the portrait had mesmerised her – it was like looking into a mirror! The glossy hair, the proud tilt of the head – it was almost identical to the portrait Piers had done of herself!

The resemblance took Lucy's breath away. Who was this Lady Sarah who looked so very much like herself? And why was the picture hung away in a disused wing of Silsbury House, as if forgotten or in disgrace? She peered intently again. 1647. That was the year before Lucy was born.

Suddenly a footfall behind her made her turn. Her heartbeat faltered a second as she saw the tall, familiar figure of Piers in the doorway.

"Lucy," he said, "I've been looking for you everywhere. I tracked you down by your footprints. How are you, Lucy?"

"I am well, thanks to you," she replied. "And you?"

She scanned his face anxiously. There were blistered scars on his face and stubbly hair about his forehead, and he still looked haggard and lined. He came into the chamber and stood before her.

"Your beautiful hair," he said in a low voice, raising his hand and fingering a limp tress that lay over her shoulder, "all blackened, all burned. Oh, my poor Lucy!"

"I am alive, and Elizabeth's babe too; but for you 't would have been more than my hair that was burned," she said.

Piers looked at her quickly. "You have not told Elizabeth of this?" Lucy shook her head, and he breathed a sigh. "She is under the impression that you had already escaped with the child by the time I arrived. I could not tell her otherwise..."

"That but for God's grace her son and her friend were already consumed by the fire? No, you could not. I would fain tell her of your bravery, but she is already convinced you are a fine man." Lucy looked away from his disconcerting gaze.

276

Piers put his finger under her chin and turned her face to his.

"But you are not so convinced, Lucy?"

"I have evidence of your courage on my behalf," she retorted.

"But you think me a traitor; you accused me yourself."

"I do not care what you are!" She broke away and walked to the window. Piers came up behind her and spoke softly over her shoulder.

"Lucy, I know you do not care, but nonetheless I am concerned lest you think badly of me."

She looked at him curiously. It was surprising to her that Piers, who she thought cared little of her opinion, should be so concerned to clear himself to her. She was proud that he considered her sufficiently important to do so, but she knew that his motives no longer concerned her. She loved him whatever he might have done. Had he not proved his strength, his determination and his courage?

"If you will permit me to explain," Piers said quietly. There was a note of question in his voice, but as Lucy did not intervene he went on. "The King has many friends yet in France whom he has known since the days of his exile. In these days of dissension between our country and France it is not easy to communicate with them, and His Majesty employs several of his trusted servants as messengers to France. Toby and I have performed this service for him on a few occasions, and such a one was the letter I entrusted to you. At that time I had reason to believe I was being watched."

Lucy could not refrain from interrupting. "Then why did you burn it later?"

"A moment," Piers replied. "The letter was concerning a certain young lady who had been a ... close friend of the King's in his exiled youth. She was of humble birth, and had written to tell him that she was to be married to a wealthy merchant, if she could find a large enough dowry. On the strength of the love His Majesty had once had for her, and on account of the child she had borne him, she begged him to help her."

Piers paused in his story. Lucy saw he was watching her face closely. "The King with his usual impulsive generosity, sent that letter to King Louis, authorising him to endow the lady with a large sum of money in his name, which he would repay King Louis. Then it came to light that the lady was in fact already wed, and had never borne the King a child at all. Our sovereign is in desperate straits already with his financial affairs, and was much relieved not to have to provide the many thousands of pounds the young lady had demanded, so I was despatched to try to stop the letter of authority from reaching King Louis.

"So you see why I was glad, Lucy, that you had not delivered it."

"Thank you for telling me," Lucy said simply.

Piers was silent a moment, his eyes downcast, then he looked up. "It is very important to me that you think well of me, Lucy," he said. "For I must tell you that I love you. I think I have always loved you..."

Slowly, disbelievingly, Lucy turned and looked at him, wide-eyed.

"From the first moment I saw you in the Tabard so long ago, I was struck by your beauty. That hair ... your eyes ... I have been cruel to you, hurtful, scornful – I know. But then I found myself painting your portrait because your face haunted me..."

Lucy felt her skin flush with excitement, and her ribs felt as though they would not be able to contain the pounding of her heart. But then she recalled how he had believed her a whore and had ridiculed the idea of defending her honour. She jutted her chin defiantly.

" 'T was a pity the object of your fascination was but a whore," she said coldly, and instantly she saw Piers' face flush.

"I am sorry. I misjudged you long ago, but you soon proved me wrong, and I have never since questioned your honour, Lucy," he said quietly.

"Indeed? The day of the duel with the Count, you and Toby found it monstrously amusing that you had been about to fight on my behalf, and not on Elizabeth's," Lucy reminded him. "The echo of your laughter could be heard the length of Hyde Park."

She turned quickly away, but despite the rustle of her skirts she heard his low reply.

"There is the laughter that is born of amusement, Lucy, and that which is but the natural release of tension when one has been under stress."

Lucy turned to face him. "My relief at not having to fight on with the Count when he discovered his mistake thrust all thoughts of others, even of you, Lucy, out of my mind," he confessed, "for he is accounted the finest swordsman in Europe, and it was but a matter of time before he would have pierced me through.

"I thought my final hour had come," he recalled, smiling ruefully. "That, and that alone, was the reason for my relief, and in my relief, my laughter."

His reaction, thought Lucy, remembering her own feelings, was now understandable and she realised he had not been ridiculing her after all. Now she too felt the happiness of relief and pure joy bubbling up inside her.

It was sufficient that she loved him, he had declared his love for her, and there was no longer any obstacle between them. Except for one thing – the difference in their birth.

Piers was standing patiently, his dark eyes searching hers. Suddenly she remembered the portrait of Lady Sarah. Perhaps Piers would know who she was. She pointed to the picture over the fireplace.

"Look, Piers, do you not see something familiar about that face?" she asked.

Piers looked up, and she saw the incredulity on his face. "By 'r lady," he exclaimed softly.

"Who is she, this Lady Sarah? Do you know?"

"Lady Sarah," he repeated thoughtfully. "Yes, I had almost forgotten. It was so long ago, and I was but a boy at the time."

"Who was she, Piers? One of Toby's family?"

"His aunt, his mother's younger sister. She died when she was very young, not yet twenty and Toby was but nine or ten years of age. We were close friends even then, so I dimly remember the scandal and how the family tried to keep the matter a secret."

"What scandal? What secret?"

Lucy felt her heart bounding in excitement. Something of import lay in this secret, she felt sure, but she knew not why she should feel such a surge of anticipation. Piers thought for a moment.

"I remember now. All Toby and I knew at the time was that Sarah, always so full of life and high spirits, had died suddenly. It was some years before we learnt the whole story from Toby's old nurse. It seems Sarah had refused all the suitors her parents had in mind for her, and given her favours to a lover of her own choice. He was as well-known as she, but unfortunately he was already married. Her parents only discovered her secret when she told them she was with child.

"Then when Sarah died in childbirth, her parents were heartbroken. The child was healthy and would only serve as a permanent reminder of their daughter's disgrace, so they decided to foster it out. Thus they tried to forget and keep their daughter's shame a secret from the rest of the world. Toby and I would never have known but for the old nurse who attended the birthing."

"And the babe?" Lucy asked.

"The family fostering it moved away and Sarah's parents lost track of them. But it mattered little to them. They did not wish to be reminded of Sarah's misfortune."

So that was why the portrait had been relegated to a little-used chamber. Lucy's mind was racing. Molly had saved her from a fire as a baby. She knew naught of the family who had just come to live in Butcher's Row – was it possibly they were not Lucy's true parents, but only fostering her? Was it possible she was the lost child? She looked at Piers and saw his eyes were scanning her closely.

"The babe – was it a maid?" she asked timidly.

Piers was smiling at her. "You know it was," he said, "and we both know that the babe was you, Lucy. Without knowing any more, it is sufficient to see you and this portrait side by side. The resemblance is breathtaking."

After a momentary pause he added, "And it would explain so much else besides. No doubt your resemblance to your mother was the reason why Toby was instantly attracted to you in the Tabard, without knowing it. And it would also explain the refinement of your features, and your natural grace and bearing."

He looked at Lucy soberly. "Can you ever forgive me, Lucy, for the abominable way I have treated you?" he asked.

"There is nothing now to forgive – and you saved my life," she reminded him. She lowered her eyes.

"Damnation!" he exclaimed. "I don't want your gratitude, woman, I want your love!" He gripped her by the shoulders. The black brows met in a furious frown over his flashing dark eyes, then his expression softened. "In any event, I too am indebted to you for saving my brother's wife and child, so the score is evened. It is odd, is it not, that babe is a veritable child of fire, just like you, my darling, born of the flames."

He turned Lucy towards him. She felt him take her hands in a strong, possessive grip as he said softly, "But just as you did, my dearest love, London will rise again from the ashes, like a phoenix, and grow even